Death Crashes the Wedding

David Q. Hall

Printed in the United States of America
First Printing 2017
All rights reserved.

ISBN 13: 978-1-948894-03-6
ISBN10: 1-948894-03-3

Copyright © 2019 by David Q. Hall

Tree Shadow Press
www.treeshadowpress.com

DEDICATION

This book is dedicated to all of the amazing, beautiful people I have been privileged to meet and know in my life's journey - whether "straight," lesbian, bisexual, gay, transgender, questioning, or just wondering why identity and private lives should matter at all in how we value others.

Everyone is a unique child of God.

ACKNOWLEDGMENTS

My sincere gratitude goes to all of the kind people who have seemed to agree that of course a retired pastor could write murder mysteries. I am particularly grateful to all of the people who have bought and read the first in the series *Death Most Unholy*, which I titled *Death Comes to the Rector*.

Some of them have been impatient and kept asking,
"When do I get the second one?"

Here it is.

PROLOGUE

The Angel of Death easily sped up the front walk of the church as quickly as the approaching bullet. The .308, 168-grain, boat-tailed bullet ripped through the voluminous sleeve of Danny's pulpit robe from the back as he put his arm around her. The bullet struck her in the upper torso and tore soft flesh through and through.

The angel invisibly gathered the exiting soul in what seemed like a vessel, scooping up a lone drop as it fell from the body...if it were possible to give bodily form to the purely spiritual event. The angel and the soul swept instantly into the timelessness of Eternity, into the spiritual Kingdom of Heaven, before the dead shell of the victim had even struck the walk and lawn below it.

As the bullet struck, the sharp *crack* of the rifle was heard across the street and up the hillside from the front of the church. Mere reflex caused Danny to look that way. At the top of the hill there was a gas station convenience store.

At the same time, he grabbed for her as she began to topple. For a split second he thought he saw a man scramble into a pickup truck that was at least a couple hundred yards away. There was something familiar about that man.

His attention returned quickly to her bleeding body as she slumped down to the grass next to the walk.

Wedding guests stood around in fear and confusion. Some ran for their cars. Some gathered around the bloody scene. Others practically froze in place, looking as though they were trying to figure out what was happening.

Down the block, Pittsburgh police officers heard the shot from their squad car. They looked toward the sound of the commotion and saw the chaotic crowd in front of the church. They stashed their to-go cups and drove to the church quickly with lights flashing and a blast of siren.

Danny motioned for those nearest to make room for the officers, who had already called for backup and emergency vehicles.

One of the wedding guests, a physician, quickly stepped forward. The others gave her room to work. Police officers moved people back while scanning the hill above with their weapons drawn, ready to respond if there was further shooting. The pickup truck had already left the convenience store parking lot above them. No other possible threat could be seen.

CHAPTER ONE

*Exactly two weeks previously on
the next-to-last Saturday in August.*

The big whitetail buck came out to the roadside ditch along highway 22 in Michigan's Leelanau County to feed in the early evening coolness. The hot August sun had just set, and shadows were lengthening across the road. The buck lifted his head, his antlers still in velvet but close to full-size for the year, and for some reason he decided to cross the highway to check out the grass on the other side.

The Rev. Dr. Danny Henriks and his long-time friend Will "Tiny" Jones rounded a curve in the road to find the big deer smack in the middle of their north-bound lane. Danny was behind the wheel of his old Jeep Grand Cherokee going 55 miles per hour. There was no chance to brake in time or swerve around the buck. In the split-second available, both Danny and Tiny braced for the impact, expecting that the deer would come flying over the hood and into the windshield.

Much to their amazement, the buck seemed to leap almost straight up and over to the south-bound lane, the left-front headlamp just clicking a rear hoof. With incredible speed, the big deer scrambled across the asphalt and into the roadside brush.

"Wow," said Tiny, "that was a close one. I was sure we were going to have a couple of hundred pounds of venison in our laps."

"Or else one incredibly angry buck," Danny said with a big smile and sigh of relief.

"How'd we miss him?" Tiny asked.

"Beats me," Danny replied. "I sure didn't have enough time to do anything. And I know those deer can move awfully fast, but he just leapt out of there in a blink. I'm glad we're almost to the bed and breakfast. I could use a pour of Crown Royal Black after that."

"Make it a double for me," Tiny agreed.

The Angel of Providence and Protection continued to speed over and ahead of their Jeep. Nothing terribly bad was going to befall Danny or Tiny. The angel was, of course, invisible, like all angels almost always existing in a spectrum of light, energy and divine power beyond human ability to see, measure, or detect in any way. Its existence and presence was rarely perceived unless there was a divine reason to reveal to human senses...and then usually only by an inner, spiritual feeling rather than in physical form.

In God's right time, all human beings are called from this earthly life back to the cosmos and eternity from which they came, but for Danny and Tiny that would not be yet. The angel had given the big buck an extra boost of its natural power and agility. Its escape from the path of the Jeep struck Tiny and Danny seemed miraculous. And it was. Supernatural power or miracle is almost always expressed in the physics of the created universe as it already exists. God works through what God already has in place.

In a few more miles the two good friends arrived and checked in at the Leelanau Bed and Breakfast, where Danny had stayed two and a half years ago.

"I have to be honest, Tiny, in that while I'm glad we're

here, and safely to boot, this feels more than a little spooky for me."

"I hear ya, brother. You haven't been to this place, or to Leelanau, since that bitch Sarah almost offed ya trying to hide the murder of her husband. And I can't believe that back in your Pitt days you two were lovers. About your taste in women..." Tiny laughed.

"Well, in my defense," Danny said, "she was different way back then. Although in retrospect, she had to have been fatally flawed for a long, long time, but neither I nor apparently anyone else could see it."

"Hey, even I could see that she was really hardheaded and had to have things her way. Although I wouldn't have guessed that she was capable of murder." Tiny admitted.

"That she was, my man. That she was. I didn't mind her stubbornness most of the time, but I guess it was so deeply ingrained that she didn't mind taking a life or three to have what she wanted. But enough of her for now. Let's go up, get a good night's sleep, and get at my therapy tomorrow morning."

"Sounds good," Tiny agreed. "That's what we came for. And I'm always there for ya, Danny. Any time. Any place."

"I know you are. You've proven that more than once. Especially up here in Leelanau."

CHAPTER TWO

Despite fatigue from the long drive that day from Pittsburgh, Pennsylvania, and the frightening, draining experience of almost hitting that buck in the highway, Danny had trouble going to sleep right away. Now that they were here, he couldn't help replaying in his head his even more harrowing escape from Sarah's murderous plans.

He had not suspected that Sarah had coldly murdered her husband, the Rev. Dr. William Brand, with his own shotgun and in his study at his church, Church of the Resurrection, Episcopal, in Shadyside, Pittsburgh. Early on, the Pittsburgh police had officially pronounced Bill's death to be a suicide. Open and shut. There was no physical evidence whatsoever that would have pointed to foul play. Sarah and her family all seemed to accept that it was suicide, however unexplainable for someone as positive about his life as Bill was. Sarah's acceptance of the suicide pronouncement was, as it tragically turned out, all an act.

In addition to the disbelief that his best friend Bill Brand would ever take his own life, Danny had noticed that the shotgun that Bill supposedly used on himself just wasn't right at the scene of the murder. It had a choke tube. Bill was a meticulous target shooter who always waited to screw a choke tube into the muzzle of his Remington 1100 until just before walking out to the trap range to shoot. He never deviated. Never. There would have been absolutely no reason for him to put in a choke tube if he merely wanted to stick

4

the muzzle of the gun in his mouth to kill himself. And even if he would have, for no sensible reason, the Bill Brand Danny knew would not have been so sloppy as to screw in the tube only part-way.

For his own reasons, Danny had kept poking around, doing his own amateur investigation of Bill's death, especially since the police had decided that there was no reason to investigate it any further.

Since he didn't seem to be willing to give up and accept the indications of suicide, Sarah finally decided that she had to get Danny out of the way. She invited him to join her in traveling up to Northern Michigan, to the Brands' summer cottage on Stony Point, outside the little village of Suttons Bay, Leelanau County, with the pretense of helping her pack up Bill's things there.

The second day that they were there, at Sarah's instigation, her secret lover, Bill's Assistant Rector, Father Frank Lewis, attacked Danny from behind. He knocked Danny unconscious and held him captive, duct-taped to a dining room chair.

Sarah planned on putting a bullet in Danny's head, then dumping him far out in the cold, dark waters of Grand Traverse Bay that night. Frank had no idea of the rest of her plan, which was to allow water to seep into the boat they were going to use, leaving him, a poor swimmer, to drown while she swam back to shore.

The final step in her murderous intent was to return to Pittsburgh in the car that Frank had used to get to Michigan and ditch it in her garage there. The next day she planned to fly one-way to Samoa to live the rest of her years in luxury on the millions of family inheritance her late husband had stashed in numbered accounts in the Caymans. She expected to be untouchable by the American justice system because there was no extradition treaty between the U.S. and Samoa.

She had almost gotten away with it. As unwitting Frank was in the process of trying to wrestle the bound Danny into the Brand boathouse and onto the boat for his final journey, Tiny and his "boy" Speed had arrived all the way from Pittsburgh in Tiny's black Lincoln. Tiny subdued Sarah with one swift punch, knocking the .38 revolver out of her hand; Speed tackled Frank and pinned him helpless to the ground, and the Leelanau County Sheriff's deputies had arrived immediately after to take control of the crime scene.

Danny and Sarah had both been taken to the hospital for their concussion symptoms. Frank, Tiny and Speed had been taken to the Leelanau County lockup. But the next day Tiny and Speed were released as their innocence of what had been going on was readily established. The day after that, Danny was released from the hospital. Speed then helped Danny gather up his things from the bed and breakfast where he had stayed for one night while trying to help Sarah, and Tiny and he had driven Danny and his Grand Cherokee and the Lincoln back to Pittsburgh.

Before long, Danny had returned to his pastoral duties at South Presbyterian Church in Pittsburgh. Eventually, both Frank and Sarah were tried and convicted. Frank was sentenced to a lengthy incarceration at the Ionia Correctional Facility in Ionia, Michigan, for his part in the attack on Danny and his unlawful imprisonment there in Michigan. Sarah had received a life sentence at the State Correctional Facility for the most serious female offenders in Muncy, Pennsylvania.

CHAPTER THREE

While Danny had gotten back to his normal life and work in many respects, over the last two and a half years he had experienced flashbacks and nightmares of his near-fatal experience in the Brand summer home. When the flashbacks didn't seem to go away on their own, he finally sought counseling and therapy. He was surprised when his therapist in Pittsburgh, Linda Mulligan, advised that he consider revisiting the scene of the crime.

"Oh, no," Danny protested. "Why would I want to go back there?"

"Frankly," she answered, "I think that the flashbacks and nightmares are a manifestation of post-traumatic stress disorder, the same sort of PTSD that soldiers and marines experience when they return from a war zone. You have stress and images that remain unresolved for you, which need closure."

"How would going back there to Leelanau County help with that?"

"Among other things," Linda explained, "by revisiting the scene of your captivity there, you can see that it's all in the past. The scene may even be different by now, not the same terrifying memory you still hold on to. And have you not told me that there were many things you liked about the area, how uniquely beautiful and lush it is?"

"Well, sure. I mean, it was great, thoroughly enjoyable up until Frank attacked me, and Sarah and he held me captive with plans to murder me. The Leelanau Peninsula is a very special place in a number of respects."

"And by actually being there again and seeing the former Brand cottage," Linda went on, "you can resolve the traumatic images in your head. You can realize that the whole place is back to being peaceful and beautiful, reinforcing those good memories you still have. It has to be your decision, Danny, but closure for those old, highly-negative memories and creating new, positive ones should be healing and strengthening for you."

"I guess that makes sense," Danny agreed. "I certainly would like more positive images to replace those flashbacks and the anxiety I occasionally experience."

"Oh," Linda added, "it would also be a good idea if you had someone who could go with you to be supportive and encouraging. It's not something you have to do alone. It's always helpful to have a strong partner when you face the anxiety you feel."

"And I know just the guy," Danny became enthused. "In fact, his specialty is providing protection services. And he's the one who saved me from that potentially fatal end up there."

"Sounds perfect."

"I fear no evil when Tiny is with me," Danny chuckled and continued. "Just as I can walk through the valley of the shadow of death when I know God is with me."

It was exactly the confidence he should have had, for there with his therapist and everywhere Danny went, the Angel of Providence and Protection continued to watch over and ahead of him. And a few weeks later, Danny and Tiny set off on the next-to-last Saturday of August for their end-of-summer road trip back to Northern Michigan.

CHAPTER FOUR

On Sunday morning, after the delicious breakfast that Leelanau Bed and Breakfast was famous for, Danny and Tiny drove the few miles over to Stony Point outside the popular tourist town of Suttons Bay. Tiny was driving the Jeep, since Danny had to admit that he was, in fact, feeling bit nervous about going back to the Brand summer home Seeing the region's beauty for the first time since his captivity seemed to help his mood. He was surrounded by the woods, lakes, cherry and apple orchards, vineyards and wineries, small organic farms and quaint villages of the Leelanau Peninsula and its gently rolling terrain. All of these reminded him of the best this part of the world had to offer.

A friend and colleague in the area had once described the entire Grand Traverse Bay region to him as "the front porch of heaven" for all its beauty and natural wonder, and it was an apt designation. If only Linda was right. He could get the images of hell he had attached to the area out of the back of his mind. He practiced the breathing exercises that Linda had taught him as they turned on to Stony Point Road and soon approached the chateau-like Brand lake cottage on West Grand Traverse Bay.

As they drove through the woods on the couple of winding turns down the driveway, the lovely, four-bedroom summer home the Brands had called "the cottage" came into clear view. And, already Linda was right. Sarah's older brother Ken and her sister Sally had acted with power of attorney to sell the home after Sarah had been convicted and incarcerated at the Muncy Correctional Facility. The new owners, a wealthy couple from suburban Detroit, had given the exterior a new coat of paint, changing the color from its old forest green and brown to a brighter yellow with brown trim and shutters.

When Tiny parked the Jeep off to the side of the garage, they were able to look down over the backyard toward the shore. Right away Danny saw that the old boathouse was gone. It was at the door going into the boathouse that he had engaged in his last, desperate struggle with Frank to somehow break free and avoid being forced into the boat for the intended last trip of his life. The new owners kept their tall sailboat at the Suttons Bay Marina and had no use for the boathouse. Besides, for many years, the Michigan State Department of Natural Resources had encouraged removal of the old boathouses from the shores of the state's thousands of inland lakes and the great lakes.

In addition to many boathouses being in disrepair and even collapse, and thus being eyesores, the importance of restoring shorelines to natural native vegetation was emphasized for the sake of wildlife and birds, and to combat erosion and pollution. It was indeed a much more peaceful and attractive scene that could now replace the ugly one that had lodged in Danny's memory. There was no place of extreme danger on that shoreline for him to fear any longer. It was one little detail of healing, but that's the way healing occurs. One step, one bit, at a time.

Danny had obtained names and phone numbers of the

new owners from the real estate office that handled the sale and purchase, and he had called the folks the previous week to ask if he and Tiny could stop by briefly and meet them and look at the home. He didn't go into his traumatic experience there two and a half years previously, figuring that the realtor who sold the house to them probably didn't use kidnapping, captivity, and planned murder as selling points. Instead, he told them that he knew the previous owners, that he had been at the house before, and that he merely wanted to see it again on his current trip. The new owners weren't going to be up north this weekend, but they said, sure, feel free to walk around the grounds and look.

"Does look different here," Tiny said. "Wonder if they've redecorated inside as well?"

"Well," Danny replied, "they said to feel free to look around, so I'll just peer in a window." He cupped his hands around his eyes and practically pressed his nose against the glass of one of the big floor-to-ceiling windows on the bay side of the house.

"The granite kitchen island and hickory flooring are still there, but I can see that they've repainted the interior also," he reported to Tiny. "The kitchen cabinets are painted white instead of natural oak, and the walls are a bright, light orange instead of the darker tan the Brands used to have. The big, old dining table and chairs the Brands had are gone, of course, and have been replaced by a more modern-style set."

Danny felt surprisingly uplifted by that last observation especially. It hadn't occurred to him really, but flashbacks to his captivity in the house for many hours often centered on his being bound to that dining room chair by duct tape, the constrained position and inability to move arms and legs having caused agonizing cramping of his muscles. Even when Sarah and Frank had lifted him up and forced him to stagger toward the boathouse to get rid of him, Danny had felt a strange gratitude to be out of the chair at least.

"So, what do you think? How does it feel to see the place again?" Tiny asked.

"You know what," Danny had to admit, "I think it does help somehow. I mean, I suppose the real impact and any long-term benefit will take time to determine, but yeah, it does seem better to know that it's not really the same place anymore. And that what happened is past and gone, and there's absolutely no reason to feel anxious and afraid anymore."

"Then let's blow this joint. I didn't feel right the first time I was here, rescuing your sorry ass. It's too fancy for this inner-city boy. Let's drive up to Suttons Bay. My mouth is watering for that fish fry lunch you promised when we got here. They serve catfish?"

Danny laughed, "No, Tiny, this isn't Southwestern Pennsylvania or inner-city Pittsburgh. The restaurant menus up here feature some of the best fresh-water, locally-caught fish you can find anywhere. Whitefish from Lake Michigan. Walleye. Lake perch. Even those crunchy, delicious little smelt. Not that there's anything wrong with your old, favorite catfish, but you're going to love fish dinners here in Northern Michigan. We should stay long enough for you to try them all. Do a comparison test," he laughed again.

Tiny thought it was good to hear his good friend Danny laugh again. The distracted, darker moods that he had exhibited from time to time over the last couple of years didn't seem to belong to the Danny whom Tiny had known for so many years. Danny was always a man of faith, hope, optimism, and good cheer that had won him over back when Tiny had wanted to chase him out of the Hill District neighborhood for "not belonging" there.

"You got my mouth watering already, Danny. Come on, I

got the keys, so I'll drive."

"Okay," Danny smiled, "just don't go twenty over the speed limit and get pulled over by a sheriff's car, like you did last time, or you won't get to that fish fry as soon as you want."

"Hey, that wasn't me; that was Slick driving. Well, okay, I told him to drive like a bat out of hell, and to take off and leave that deputy back in his car, doing his license check, but damned good thing we did."

"You're right there," Danny had to admit. "A minute or two later and those two would have had me loaded up on that boat and out on the dark water. And you wouldn't have been able to swim after us fast enough to catch up and save me."

They both roared with laughter. "You're damn right about that," Tiny agreed. "These 310 pounds of magnificent black manhood may float like an island in the 'Y' pool back in Pittsburgh, but it sure isn't built for swimming races. I would have just stood in the night on that shore and hollered, 'Okay, you can have him. I'm going for fish fry.'"

Tears of happiness rolled down both their cheeks as they laughed so hard that Tiny practically had to pull over to the side of the road and stop the Jeep. Without saying a word, they each had the same thought, *Damn, this is good.* Healing and laughter are always good.

CHAPTER FIVE

A hungry Tiny did, in fact, push the Grand Cherokee a bit over the posted speed limit, and in a matter of minutes the two of them were seated at a table in the VI Grill in downtown Suttons Bay. Danny recommended to Tiny that he try the locally-caught whitefish, tossing in the bit of trivia that Danny had read that the Native Americans of the far north, specifically the Inuit and Cree, loved whitefish so much that they would save it for their own consumption, throwing salmon and char to their sled dogs to eat. He ordered the same.

The filets were large, but Tiny gobbled them down quickly. He didn't mind that it was not all-you-can-eat. He ordered a second batch.

"Man, you're right. This is delicious. I think you also had it right that we should stay long enough for me to try all the other kinds of fish. If they're anywhere near as good as this, I may just have to move here myself."

"But what about 'Big Tiny's Protection Services' and your other Pittsburgh businesses?" Danny kidded him. "You just going to retire and turn it all over to Speed and Slick?"

"Don't people up here need protection and security?"

"I'm sure some of these big, fancy, waterfront homes do have security systems at least. Leelanau County has the highest average property values of all the 83 counties in the State of Michigan, and the owners wouldn't want to take chances on possible break-ins and burglaries. On the other hand, it's a really low-crime area, so I don't know how much business you could drum up."

"Well," Tiny said, "it's a beautiful place and has great places to eat, and man, I just love this fish." They both laughed with delight.

"You said you wanted to go over to that Cedar Rod & Gun Club this afternoon to do some target shooting?" he asked Danny.

"Yeah, I think that would be fun. When I stopped by there two and a half years ago, trying to figure out whether Bill's death was a suicide or possibly a murder, they had made me feel really welcome. John Harrison, the famous gun fitter and stock bender invited me to return there and shoot as a guest any time. Do you want to go with me?"

Tiny laughed again. "An inner-city boy like me? All I ever knew was handguns with filed-off serial numbers and an occasional Mac-10. Never shot with no shotguns. Well, that's not quite right. In my miscreant days as a street hood, there was one time when I wrestled a sawed-off out of the hands of a shop owner. Damn fool thought he could scare us off and save a couple of hundred dollars in his till. I fired that gun right into the ceiling as a warning not to mess with us, and *he* was the one who was scared," Tiny chuckled.

Danny sat across from him at the table with a look of disbelief.

"What?" Tiny asked. "You shocked that I was such a bad-ass all those years ago? I've reformed, you know, put all that punk stuff behind me long ago."

"No," Danny explained. "I just can't believe you just used

a fifty-cent word like 'miscreant.'"

They both roared, and the nearby customers turned and looked at the two with smiles. It's always good to see people having fun and laughing.

Finally, able to settle down and get some words out again, Danny asked, "So what do you want to do while I'm at the shooting range?"

"You know," Tiny said, "I think I'm just going to walk around the main drag here, look in some of these shops. There's a kind of funky-looking place across the street that has a sign for Case knives in the window. Maybe I can finally replace my old switchblade that those sheriff deputies confiscated back on the night we rescued you."

"Oh, that's right," Danny said. "They never gave that back to you. Probably ended up in somebody's crime weapon collection."

"And I'm curious about those signs that say 'Leland Blue' and 'Petoskey Stones.' What are those, anyway?"

Danny bit his tongue. He was infamous for launching into lectures on all kinds of trivial information at every opportunity but decided that he would let Tiny do his own inquiries and not spoil his fun.

"Well, why don't you explore a little bit and find out? I'll be back to pick you up here towards 4:00 if that sounds good."

Tiny agreed. They paid their bill, and Danny drove off, leaving Tiny standing outside VI Grill, looking up and down the street at the brightly-colored shops, souvenir places, ice cream stands, several restaurants, small art galleries, a funeral home and the only gasoline station/convenience store in Suttons Bay. It sure was different than the squalid, dirty streets of the Hill District in Pittsburgh, the old slum-ghetto where he had lived all his life. But he liked it here in Leelanau County, Michigan. Maybe approaching sixty was a good time to think about retirement, after all.

He decided to cross the street – which was also Highway 22 going up the east coast of the Leelanau Peninsula – and see about those Case knives in the funky-looking gift shop. Immediately another difference from his old Pittsburgh neighborhood became evident. Since Tiny was standing in the beginning of a crosswalk, oncoming traffic from both north and south actually slowed and stopped for him, and on a state highway.

"People here are remarkably courteous," he smiled to himself. "Or else they're worried about the possible damage to their bumpers and grills if they hit someone my size. Yah, probably the latter," he laughed. He entered the shop but never made it to the knife display.

CHAPTER SIX

Although there were a few tourists in the gift shop that Sunday afternoon, the woman at the cash register wasn't occupied with anyone at that moment. She was looking down, sorting through some papers, and didn't see Tiny come in. He, on the other hand, couldn't see anything *but* her. Tiny had been with many women in his years – once a stunning African-American model in Pittsburgh – but he had never beheld such beauty in his entire life. She was mesmerizing.

Angela McGinty was five foot-ten and in her early fifties. As a much younger woman she had possessed a natural beauty that would have driven runway models into fits of jealousy, and the passing years had only mellowed and burnished that loveliness with soft lines around her eyes and mouth. Her naturally-tightly-coiled hair was a dark auburn, and the slight streaks of gray acted like natural highlights that only served to make it more attractive. Her skin appeared considerably more youthful than her age, smooth, tight, and beautifully light-olive in shade. And although her figure was not quite as slim as it had been in her twenties and thirties, she was still very shapely and, well, sexy.

The browsing tourists still shuffled around the displays of the store, so Tiny approached the counter where Angela was standing. Never in his almost-sixty years had *anyone* intimidated Tiny. Not gigantic linemen on the football field. Not the toughest gang members on the Hill. Not squads of armed policemen. Certainly not the mayor and councilmen of Pittsburgh. But now he felt the nervousness of an adolescent boy working up his courage to talk to a girl he liked. And what was that little bit of weakness in his knees? Probably from his old football injuries. Yah, that was probably it.

He opened his mouth and couldn't believe that an almost-stammer came out.

"Ah, ah, I wanted to ask..."

Angela looked up with a radiant smile that almost knocked Tiny over.

"Good afternoon. How may I help you?"

"Ah, well, I'm new to this area, and I wondered, could you tell me what Petoskey stones are? I see signs about them all over around here."

"Fossilized coral from ancient coral reefs going back, oh, about 350 million years ago, the Devonian Period," Angela explained. "The coral animals formed hexagonally-shaped cells or tubes, died, and when they were buried under sand and silt, over time the organic material was replaced with mineral deposits – 'fossilization.' Eventually chunks of the fossil rock were broken off, dragged and scraped and often rounded by the glaciers that covered Northern Michigan in the Ice Ages, and then deposited in the sands and moraines that help make this area as beautiful as it is."

She held up a particularly large Petoskey stone and pointed out the hexagonal pattern in the brown-grey, polished stone. "You see the beautiful markings. The geologists call the stone 'Hexagonia percarinate' because of this distinct pattern. Lapidaries cut and polish the stones to bring out the shine and the colors. Gemologists and jewelry designers set the polished stones in all kinds of jewelry items. Knick-knacks, bookends, paper weights, all kinds of things are made out of them or with them. They're unique to this area along the Northwestern Michigan lakeshore, and the City of Petoskey up the coast, on the way to Mackinac and The Bridge, seems to be central to the region in which the stones are found."

She gently placed the large Petoskey stone in the palm of Tiny's huge hand for him to examine it more closely. Was it his imagination, or did her soft touch linger for a second before she withdrew her hand gracefully? Whatever, he felt like he had been brushed by an angel, and he had heard the most fascinating mini-lecture on geology and lapidaries he had ever heard in his life, not that he was sure he had even heard the term "lapidary" ever before. And all delivered with a smile and a twinkle in her eyes that seemed to him as though they could melt mountains far faster than any glacier could grind them down. His stammer eased a bit as he smiled back like a shy little boy.

"City of Petoskey, eh? Named after the stones?"

"Oh, no," Angela corrected, "the city is named after a famous Ottawa – or Odawa – Native American chief who lived with his people in that region along the Lake Michigan coast. His name was 'Pet-O-Sega,' which the white settlers pronounced 'Petoskey.' The stones are named after the city, the area, and, in a way, after the chief."

Maybe the most beautiful woman I've ever met, and damn smart, too, Tiny thought. While Angela turned to take care of a tourist couple who were ready to pay for their purchases, he worked up his courage to ask her out. But she beat him to it. They no more than exchanged names by way of introduction when she said,

21

"How would you like to buy a girl a latte, big boy? It's 2:00, and I have a 15-minute break coming." She flashed that radiant smile. "And I bet my boss would give me 30; wouldn't you, Sam?"

Sam waved her out as he continued to show a customer a Swiss Army knife he had taken out of a locked case in the back of the store. Angela grabbed her purse from under the counter and headed out the door as if she knew Tiny would be right behind her. And he was...as surely as if he had been on a leash.

CHAPTER SEVEN

Within minutes Tiny and Angela were seated at a table in the 45th Parallel Café, she with her requested Chai Tea latte, and he with a big mug of black coffee.

"So, Tiny, would you like to hear more about Petoskey stones?" she said teasingly.

Starting to relax a bit more, Tiny countered with probably a bit too much eagerness, "Actually, I'd like to hear more about you, Angela. Have you lived in this area for long?"

"Just for a couple of years. I grew up in Los Angeles and lived there for most of my life. My father was a South Central native; his mother was Samoan and French; his father, African-American and Irish. My mother was Native American on her mother's side – Apache, and Spanish on her father's side. I guess I'm a funny kind of mixture and seemed to fit there in the most multi-cultural, multi-ethnic, multi-lingual city in the world."

"Heinz 57 varieties," Tiny chimed in. Angela looked a bit quizzical. "That's what we always said in Pittsburgh where I was born and still live. It's the home of the big Heinz Company, you know, ketchup and all that." He grinned broadly and held up the Heinz ketchup bottle sitting at the back edge of their table. At the same time, Angela's brief explanation of her ancestry and biography struck a resonating chord with Tiny.

He knew that South Central had long been a large African-American neighborhood on the south side of Los Angeles and was infamous for being the heart of the South Central riots in the spring of 1992. They were often called the "Rodney King Riots" because of the brutal and excessive beating of Rodney King, an African-American construction worker, in March of 1991 by four Los Angeles police officers. But Tiny also knew that the riots and the fifty-three deaths that occurred from their violence and destruction had also stemmed from a long history of troubled race relations and discrimination and neglect of that part of the city by politicians and authorities. It was a challenging place in which to grow up, and many young people never made it to adulthood, or if they did, never managed to escape the poverty and problems of South Central. It was a lot like being born and growing up in the Hill District of Pittsburgh as Tiny did.

"So how did you happen to move here all the way from South Central?" Tiny asked.

Angela laughed, "That's what people always ask me. What brought me from sunny and warm Southern California to the cold and snowy winters of Northern Michigan. They don't always come right out and say it, but from their expressions you know they're thinking, 'Are you nuts or something?'"

Both of them chuckled at that, and Tiny felt like he was listening to the voice of an angel, so smitten he was. Angela continued.

"Well, we were pretty poor, my family and I, when I was growing up in Los Angeles, but one possession I had was the ability to sing and the perfect pitch that God had given me. I used to sing all the time in the choir at our Baptist church, and in the choral group of my high school in South Central. One year I won a regional high school talent show, and the grand prize was an all-expense-paid scholarship to the National Music Camp at Interlochen, Michigan, just south of here a little way. It was so much fun – kids and instructors from all over the country, all over the world, actually, including quite a few from California – that when I got back home in the slum, I started doing fund raising projects so that I could go back the next summer."

"And you made it back?"

"Yes, thankfully. It takes thousands of dollars just to attend there for a summer program, but a lot of people helped me out: my high school choir director, my wonderful choir members at church, our pastor, Reverend Black. So, I went back the next summer, the summer before I graduated, and loved it even more, just loved this whole beautiful area."

Tiny smiled broadly at her gushing enthusiasm. "But that had to be a couple of years ago. What took you so long to relocate to this place you fell in love with?"

"You flatterer," Angela waved her hand at him. "Well, I was young and foolish, and thought that I was in love, so right out of high school I lived with this fellow there in South Central. He was a junkie and a pusher who talked big, like he owned the streets and the crack trade there, and he was going to make big money and buy me a beach home in Malibu, live among the movie stars. But I was too blind to see that the only thing big about him was the size of loser he was. I waited tables and worked extra shifts to support us while he smoked and shot up and spent most of his days in a haze, rather than a job."

"Believe me, Angela, I know that story far too well. I hope it won't scare you off, but I'll be upfront right off and tell you that years ago I fell into a similar trap back on the Hill in Pittsburgh. Thank God and my sponsor – and I praise them both every day of my life – I kicked that habit and lifestyle through Narcotics Anonymous." Tiny reached in his pants pocket and brought out a little medallion. "Still recovering, but clean and sober 34 years, seven months, one week, and today. One day at a time."

"Wow, that's great. What an accomplishment, really."

"I had to have a guardian angel looking over me all that time," Tiny said. "'Cause I don't think I could have done it just on my own power. It was still all around me, tempting me, every day on the Hill in Pittsburgh. Every day I wondered if I would be given enough strength for that day. So, you never married that fellow?"

"No, I mean, I wanted to; thought he would be my life partner, despite his addictions and his fantasy world delusions. But he OD'd one day when he had been gone on a high for days, me not knowing where he was, what alley or crack house he had disappeared to. It just tore me up at the time, but looking back, I think God saved me from maybe eventually sliding into his inescapable pit."

"Damn...oh, I'm sorry." It was probably the first time ever that Tiny had apologized for little bit of profanity, but he felt a tremendous need inside to do, and be, and speak, in the right way for this wonderful woman. Angela smiled with a touch of amusement as he continued. "I, I'm really sorry," Tiny stammered a bit, "that you had to go through that heartache. So. Have you ever been married?" Immediately he wondered if he was being too intrusive asking that, but Angela didn't seem to mind a bit, and readily answered.

"Yes, years later when I was in my early 30's I met a talented jazz musician at a night club in Los Angeles. Never having the opportunity or means to go to college, I was still waiting tables, serving with a smile for tips from clubbers who had too much money, drank too much, and wanted to take the waitress out to the back for a quickie. But he was different. He loved music like I did, and when his jazz band played at the club, it was all I could do not to dump a tray of drinks in some jerk's lap, take his seat when he went to complain to the manager, and just sit there and listen to Mack's clarinet until I got fired and had to leave. Wow, I guess I've just revealed *my* dark side," Angela laughed.

"After about four months of his playing at the club in scheduled gigs, and over three months of him and me dating, he convinced me to go to the courthouse and get married. I had always dreamed of a church wedding, you know, at my Baptist church, with my dear choir members singing, and Reverend Black officiating. But once again I thought I was in love, and whatever he wanted, it was fine with me."

Tiny obviously wanted to ask her something but practically squirmed to keep from saying it. Angela recognized his discomfort and went on with a twinkle in her eyes.

"You're wondering what happened, then, to the two of us."

Tiny cocked his head and smiled rather sheepishly, again like a teenage boy, "Yah, you got me."

"Truth is, I loved his music and his attention, what we had in common. But I don't think he ever really loved me. Oh, he loved having someone to be at home for him, to cook and clean and take care of things for him; pay the bills, put in more shifts when he was between gigs and wasn't bringing in any money. But I was blind to the fact that from the beginning he was doing it with any other waitress he could sneak around with, or any woman who fell for his music and his BS. When I woke up to what was really going on, I divorced him."

Listening to Angela's difficult path through early life, Tiny was surprised at the inner pain he felt for her. It was amazing that she was willing to share such details with a guy she had so recently met, and even more, that she seemed so "together" that she could talk about it so matter-of-factly, even with a genuine smile. *This woman is remarkable,* he thought.

It seemed redundant to him to say again that he was so sorry about what had happened to her, so he decided to shift the focus to himself for a bit.

"I've never been married. I dated a lot of girls, women, that is. And I had girlfriend relationships – a couple for a year or two or three, but..."

Angela gently interrupted him, not at all shy about asking what she wanted to know.

"You never found the Right One?"

"Yah, that's probably the best way to sum it up for me. I mean, I liked, maybe even loved in a way, more than one of them, but somehow, I never found, maybe was never blessed with, the person I knew would be my life partner in everything. You know what I mean?"

"I sure do," Angela replied. "After my divorce, I was in my mid-30's by then, well, I felt like I was walking under a dark cloud all the time, like that cartoon character, what was his name, years ago in *L'il Abner*?"

"I remember," Tiny exclaimed, "Joe Btfsplk...." although even his creator, Andy Capp, couldn't pronounce the unpronounceable name, so he would always express it with a loud "raspberry," which is what Tiny did for Angela.

"Yes," she agreed, then did it herself, "Joe Btfsplk..k...kkk."

The two of them doubled over in delight and laughter.

"For some years I wondered to myself," Angela went on, "if I was just cursed by God or something. I turned my attention to saving up what money I could, started taking some courses at Cal State University of Los Angeles, and finally graduated with an Associate Degree in bookkeeping.

That enabled me to do freelance bookkeeping for people and small businesses while I continued to wait tables. Gradually I improved my situation in life; was able to get a nicer apartment, do more things than just struggle to buy enough groceries for the week. But even though I would occasionally date some guy, I was pretty guarded, twice-burned kinda, and maybe I never gave a fellow a real chance with me...or maybe just never found one I wanted to give a chance to," she shrugged.

"But how did you decide at last to leave Southern California after all those years and move up here to the land of snow and ice?"

"Hey, it's not Antarctica. Look around at this beautiful, warm August weather. Most of the trees are still green, although it's exciting to see bits of fall color showing up already. This is the land of four wonderful seasons, not like Southern California, where the seasons are variations on the same theme: hot, not quite so hot, hot again. But to answer your question, after about ten years continuing to wait tables, serve for tips, and do my bookkeeping, I felt like I wanted something different in my life. Honestly, I looked back and asked myself, when and where was I most happy in my lifetime? And it was here, when I came to Northern Michigan for those summer camps at Interlochen."

Tiny smiled broadly and said, "Well I'm really happy for you, and that you're here where I could meet you. Sure glad I walked into your shop."

"The shop," Angela gasped. "Time has gone by so quickly, we've been here over half an hour already. I better get back."

Tiny rose quickly, grabbed the check to pay, and winced a bit. "I hope I haven't gotten you in trouble with Sam, your boss."

"Na, you see, I not only work the store for him; I also keep his books. If he has any hope of understanding his receipts, expenditures, tax liabilities, and profit margin, hoping that he has one, he better keep me on," she laughed.

Tiny walked her back across the street, where once again he noted the minor miracle of cars stopping for them while they were in the crosswalk. *Sure is different here*, he noted again. At the shop, he didn't really want to leave, and stood awkwardly for a second not knowing what to do or say, but Angela came to his rescue.

"You know, we spent all that time with me talking about my history. What say I take you to dinner tonight and you tell me about Tiny Jones.... including your real first name, assuming you have one. Say, meet me back here when I get off at 6:00?"

Tiny beamed with pleasure. "I'll be here. And it's Will, by the way. But you can call me what you want." Angela gave him a gorgeous wink and a little hug, and went back to check with Sam. Tiny left, never even thinking about that replacement knife he originally went in there for but kept on thinking about Angela. *What a woman. And she's willing to pay for dinner, too.*

Tiny walked down the main street of Suttons Bay, going into a few more shops, and while he thought they were interesting, he really couldn't think about much but Angela, and how he had to wait for over three more hours to be with her again. He had most of an hour to kill before Danny would be picking him up, so he strolled over to Bahle Park, sat down on a bench, and watched with a smile as children were playing around the little creek that flowed through the park.

CHAPTER EIGHT

Upon leaving Tiny on the main street of downtown Suttons Bay, Danny made the slightly less than half-hour drive down to the Cedar Rod & Gun Club, outside the little village of Cedar in Leelanau County. He pulled into the parking lot with about an hour left in the shooting schedule for that Sunday, and figured he had enough time to get in at least one round of sporting clays. He liked both skeet and sporting clays better than trap because they both simulated the shooting challenges one might face when out in the woods, pursuing ruffed grouse or woodcock. That was especially true with sporting clays, since the course for it was laid out along a winding path through the woods, with trap machines set up at each station sending targets through and into the trees much like flushing birds in the forest.

Danny had called the previous week and talked to John Harrison of the Cedar Club, and John had told Danny that he would be delighted to shoot a round with him at the end of the shooting day on Sunday. And sure enough, when Danny walked in the door of the range house, there was John, waiting for him, and the range master, George, behind the counter as usual.

"Well, look at what the cat dragged in, and all the way from Pennsylvania," hollered John. "Get yourself ready; the last squad of shooters on sporting clays is heading back in now, so it's our turn next."

Danny smiled, delighting in the kidding, and shook hands with John. Range Master George added his own greeting.

"Dr. Henriks, er, Danny, welcome back. It's been what, a couple of years or more?"

"I'm afraid so, George, but it feels good to be back here, and to have a chance to shoot a round today."

George refrained from any reference to the captivity and intended murder that Danny had survived at the hands of Sarah Brand and her young lover, Frank Lewis. All the regular members and shooters had heard about it, including George, of course. The Leelanau Peninsula was a very small-town environment, and whatever happened, especially such exciting police action, quickly made the rounds, and got embellished and expanded along the way.

At least one version had Danny's rescue in the nick of time occurring thanks to a unit of special operations troops, capturing a band of kidnappers for ransom in an exciting shoot-out. Another version played on Danny's African-American friends, Tiny and Slick, but had an entire gang of black street thugs involved, whether as captors or rescuers there seemed some debate. So, while no one said anything out of politeness, of course, conversations in the range house quieted down considerably and all eyes turned as Danny was welcomed.

John spoke again, "Danny, I'd like to introduce you to the other three shooters who will go with us on the course today. George will come out from behind the counter to join us; this is Fred, one of our most active members and shooters." Danny and Fred shook hands. "And this is Andrea. Andrea is a Michigan State Highway Patrol officer, stationed at the

State Police Post on 14th Street over in Traverse City."

Danny hadn't even noticed Andrea Wilkins up to that point in the small crowd that rather filled the range house. Most of the male shooters were as tall as, or a bit taller than, Danny himself, while Andrea was 5'5", maybe 5'6" at most, and she had been almost hidden in the group. But as they shook hands and exchanged "Glad to meet you," Danny found himself looking into the most beautiful, sparkling blue eyes he had ever seen, accompanied by a radiant smile that seemed to light up the room.

As they gathered up shotguns and shells to head out to the sporting clays course, Danny thought right away that Andrea presented an intriguing combination for a woman: she had all the authoritative presence and demeanor you would expect from the veteran state trooper she was, ramrod posture, confident and in control, but at the same time exhibiting a natural beauty and feminine grace that was alluring. She happened to be the only woman at the club to shoot this day, and while the men obviously reacted to her with courtesy, he could also tell that they regarded her with respect and accepted her as an equal in the male-dominated environment.

In the shooting rotation that had been set up for that round Danny followed Andrea as they took their turns at each station, which gave ample opportunity to chat while waiting for the previous shooters to finish.

"Officer Wilkins," Danny asked as they stood in the back of the first station, "have you been stationed at the Traverse City Post for very long?"

"Please, it's Andrea. And yes, I've operated out of there for six, going on seven years now. I love it there. I grew up in Traverse City, so it's always been home for me."

"Is it unusual for a state trooper to get posted in their old home town? I would think it would be rather rare."

"Yes, it is. I graduated from Traverse City Central High, and then Michigan State University with a degree in criminal justice in the College of Social Science. I always wanted to be in law enforcement. My dad was a cop. Then I started out as a deputy sheriff in the small town of Baldwin, Michigan. I was there for several years, and liked it a lot, but I really had my sights set on making it into the State Police Training Academy in Lansing. I was finally accepted at the age of 32, graduated, took an initial posting downstate in the little town of Paw Paw, was there for several years, but was glad when there was an opening up here in Traverse City, got approved for a transfer, and I could actually come home."

Danny listened with great interest, meanwhile noting that her work history probably made her in her mid- to late-forties. Intrigued, he couldn't help but glance at her left hand, noting that there was no wedding band, nor a tan mark, on the ring finger.

"Do you come here to shoot often?" he asked.

"Oh, yes, especially since our post does some of our range shooting here at Cedar. The facilities are good, and the club really accommodates us. Oh, my turn."

Andrea stepped up to the station. On her command, "Pull," a mechanical trap machine flung a bright orange clay target out into an opening in the trees. She swung her over-under shotgun smoothly and quickly, shot, and the target disintegrated into small pieces and dust. At the "report" of her shot, another trap flung a second target at a different angle, crossing in front of her. Swinging her gun smoothly again from the direction of the first target's path, she swung through and ahead of the second target, shot, and another hit.

Wow, thought Danny, *bright, attractive, a strong woman, confident and professional...and she sure can shoot.* He wondered if she would accept an invitation to lunch or dinner. It was his turn next at the station. He connected crisply on the first, straightaway target, but was a little slow swinging on the tough crossing shot, missing the second target as it disappeared into the foliage to his right. He didn't mind that Andrea had shown him up on that station. He found himself attracted to her in a way he hadn't felt for who knows how many years.

Danny engaged in conversation and banter with the other shooters in their squad as they went through the course, especially John Harrison, but found himself talking to Andrea as much as possible, hoping that it wasn't too obvious to the others that he was feeling, well, fascinated with her. For her part, she asked about his life and work as well.

"I heard George address you as 'Dr.' when you first walked in. Are you a physician?"

"No," Danny replied, "George was being a little too formal, but as you know, there are lots of different kinds of 'doctors.' It's actually 'The Rev. Doctor'. I'm a Presbyterian pastor in Pittsburgh, Pennsylvania, South Presbyterian Church."

"Great," Andrea responded with enthusiasm. "I go to Grand Traverse Presbyterian Church in Traverse City. Sing in the choir every Sunday I'm not on patrol and play hand bells as often as my work schedule allows."

Danny brightened even more at that connection between them.

"Have you always been a Presbyterian, Andrea?"

"Actually, while I was growing up in Traverse City, my family and I belonged to Central Methodist, and it's a fine congregation yet today. But while I was posted in Paw Paw, I met, dated, and eventually married, a fellow there who was a lifelong resident and member of the First Presbyterian Church in Paw Paw. I really liked the church and the

Presbyterian system. There are, as you know, no bishops. It's a representative democracy the way the churches are governed, and they even elected me an elder a couple of years after we were married there, and I joined. I just liked the feeling that I could be my independent self, use my strengths and skills in the church, and be treated as equal to anybody else."

"I apologize in advance if I'm being too intrusive, but your husband and you are no longer together?"

"No problem. No, we were married and lived there in Paw Paw for about five years, but then one night when he was coming home from work at the lumber company his pickup truck was struck by a drunk driver who swerved into his lane on County Road 665. He was dead on the scene."

"Andrea, I'm so sorry."

They all completed the last station, having fired a total of 50 shots each, and Danny noticed that they had finished on the hillside overlooking the range house. Their squad of five paused right next to the 200-yard back board of the rifle range. Rifle shooting and skeet shooting were closed, of course, while sporting clays was operating, as both rifle and skeet shooters would have to fire in the direction of anyone using the sporting clays course.

As the scorekeeper was tallying up how each of them had done on their round of shooting, Danny and Andrea continued to chat, while John, George, and Fred, club members and friends for years, joked and ribbed each other about easy shots missed.

"Do you have any family?" Andrea asked Danny.

"No, not really," he replied. "My late wife, Samantha, died, oh, over 13 years ago now. We didn't have any children. Both of my parents are gone. I have a few cousins, an uncle, a couple of aunts, but I only see them every few years or so. I don't even have a cat to serve, but if I lived up here, a bird dog would be nice to take advantage of the grouse and woodcock hunting available in these forested areas."

"I agree," Andrea said with some obvious enthusiasm. "I live alone in my condo, but a bird dog would be nice if I had my own house and a yard for it."

Scores were announced for their round of shooting and sure enough, Andrea had broken four more targets than had Danny. As they were about to hike down to the range house, he gathered the courage to ask her.

"Say, are you working today? And if not, would you be available for a little supper out this evening?"

"No, I'm off this Sunday. And I don't have any plans, was just going to go back to the condo to kick back. Sure, I'll join you for a bite. How 'bout we meet at the Mackinaw Brewing Company on Front Street in Traverse City at 7:00, and I'll buy."

This woman is strong, independent, and used to being in charge, thought Danny. He liked that about her.

"Fine with me," he agreed. "Mackinaw Brewing Company at 7:00. And you'd better be prepared to pay for my big appetite," he kidded her.

Almost simultaneously the discernible puff of air between their faces, the thud of a lead bullet in the back board behind them, and the loud "crack" of a .308 rifle shattered the otherwise peaceful scene. The bullet had passed between Andrea and Danny, missing each of them by only a few inches. For a split-second it was as though the five shooters and the scorekeeper were frozen statues, but Andrea's training and experience kicked immediately into gear.

"Everybody down!" she barked, as she literally knocked Danny flat. Her eyes quickly swept the slope down to the range house. A number of men scurried around the front of the house and around the rifle benches. Mingled shouts and shoving erupted down there, and both Danny and she spotted a figure running into the parking lot and jumping into a battered, rusty, red pickup truck. It roared off, spraying gravel behind its rear wheels.

In the ongoing hubbub down there, however, a second figure slipped unseen behind the building, snuck behind the storage shed, then behind the larger club house, and eventually through an opening in the fence at the far end of the club property. The man started the car parked by itself down there and drove off quietly and unnoticed.

CHAPTER NINE

"Everybody, stay down," Andrea ordered, as she continued to survey the milling scene down near the range house. The men near her at the end of the sporting clays course resisted their mutual inclination to jump into action and stayed hunkered down as she had told them. A voice hollered up the slope from the vicinity of the house.

"Everybody okay up there?"

Andrea was quick to respond. "Yes, we're fine. Okay to come down?"

"Come on down," the voice bellowed back.

All six of them were at least a little bit shaken, but soon the squad of shooters and the scorekeeper were back at the range house. George, being the responsible range master, asked the crowd of men, "What happened down here?"

Bill, who had been left in charge while George took a turn at shooting for himself, was quick to respond.

"Gosh, George, I'm really sorry about all this. A fellow came in just after your squad started on the course. He said he was vacationing in Leelanau, was told that nonmembers were allowed to shoot at our club and wanted to practice on the rifle range to get ready for the upcoming deer season. I told him, of course, that the rifle range was closed until after sporting clays was done for the day, but that he could shoot after that."

"Did you get proper identification, and did he have a member to vouch for him?" George asked Bill.

"Yes, on both counts. Well, at least I tried to. At first, he said that he had left his wallet in his car, but would it be okay if he set his cased rifle down on a bench, along with his supply duffle, while he went to get his driver's license. I didn't see any harm at that, so I said okay. Wes Smith was alongside him and spoke up at that point saying he'd vouch for the fellow as an experienced and safe shooter."

"Wes Smith," Andrea exclaimed, rolling her eyes upward. "I've run into him before. He and his brothers are known game law violators; at least one of them has a prison record, and I've stopped Smith a couple of times on area state highways for speeding and DUI."

"Well," Bill put his hands up a bit defensively, "he is a member, and our rules say if a member vouches for a guest..."

George put a hand out to steady Bill. "It's okay, Bill, nobody's saying you done wrong here. But how did the shot occur? Have any idea?"

"I watched him set his gun and gear down at a rifle bench. He opened up the case, held up the rifle so I could see it with the chamber open and unloaded, and laid it down on the open case on the bench, muzzle pointed down range."

"You really should have told him to keep the gun cased until after everybody was in from the sporting clays course, but I know it's common for shooters to lay their guns and gear down on those rifle benches, shotgunners, too, but the shot?" George pressed.

"It looked like he was headed back out to the parking lot, you know, to get his wallet, but it got busy just then. I had four/five guys wanting to check out and pay for their shooting, end of the day, you know. A few more had already checked out but were hanging around the range house here. I think a couple of them were hoping to talk to John about adjusting the fit of their shotguns once he was back down from shooting. Two or three were still shooting the bull at the near edge of the parking lot, right outside the house. I didn't notice anyone at all over by the rifle benches. So, I," Bill stammered. "I. Well. There didn't seem to be any potential for a problem,".

"Any of you guys see anything?" George asked the crowd around the front of the range house.

"I did see that stranger over by his rifle and gear on the bench shortly before the shot occurred," one volunteered. "But it looked like he was just checking his supplies. He wasn't sitting down as if ready to shoot. But I turned away before the shot rang out."

"Well, what did you see after the shot?" Andrea jumped in.

Another answered, "Well, as soon as the rifle cracked, that Wes Smith took off from near the benches and ran across the front of the range house."

"That's right," Bill took over the discussion again, "I looked up at the shot and saw him dashing past the door here. He headed through the gate, jumped into his old, rusty pickup, and sped off."

"A couple of us in the parking lot wondered if we should have tried to stop him, but it all happened so fast."

"Did anybody see what became of the stranger and his rifle and gear after the shot and Wes took off?" Andrea asked.

Heads shook, and Bill responded, "When Wes ran out to his truck, I left my checking out those guys, stepped out the door, and I glanced over to the rifle benches, but nothing was there. And no sign of the guest shooter. He just seemed to disappear on us."

"So, you never actually got the ID?" George asked. Bill shook his head and shrugged, feeling at fault and rather negligent.

"Can you describe him?" Andrea queried. "Anything to distinguish him?"

"He was medium height, maybe late fifties, mostly grey hair, sort of average-looking, friendly fellow, mannerly...oh, and he had a bit of an accent, obviously not a native Michigander."

"How would you describe his accent?"

"Kinda soft. Just a bit of a drawl. Maybe Southerner?"

"Okay, thanks," Andrea smiled at Bill to put him at least a bit at ease. She turned back to George and Danny standing next to him.

"It may have been nothing more than an accidental discharge. Put a cartridge in the breech, worked the bolt, set it down, and it went off on impact. If he had kept it pointing down range, it would have pointed pretty much in our direction; bullet just happened to narrowly miss us. And when the gun went off, he may have been startled and scared himself, quickly gathered it and his gear bag up, and took off before anyone could question him."

"But it seems mighty suspicious," Danny suggested, "that this Wes fellow took off running in the opposite direction at that precise moment. Maybe a diversion?"

"That's certainly possible," Andrea agreed. "It's going to be hard to track down this stranger, without an ID, never actually gave his name, no description of his vehicle, certainly no license number, but for some reason Wes Smith spoke up and vouched for him. So that would be the direction I would look, as well as why Wes ran off and roared away in his truck. But it's not my jurisdiction here. It's the

Leelanau County Sheriff. So, I'll have to call them and request an investigation. I'll need to take down names and contact information for all you men, so that they can get a hold of you if they need to."

The small crowd of men all nodded and murmured assent, and Andrea passed around a tablet for them to write down names and phone numbers. While they were doing so, she put in a call to the sheriff's dispatch at the Leelanau County Administrative Center.

When things quieted down, the shooters dispersed to their vehicles. Shooting hours at the sporting clays range were over for the day. Danny spoke alone to Andrea.

"What do you think? A careless, accidental discharge, or could it have been intentional?"

"Hard to tell," she responded. "Probably accidental. Now Wes Smith and I have had a few run-ins, as I said before, but I can't believe that he would hold a murderous grudge so as to try to shoot me out there. Those Smith boys are scofflaws when it comes to state game and fish regulations, and maybe some minor thefts or break-ins to unoccupied cabins and cottages, but none of them, including Wes, have ever been arrested for a violent act. To the best of my knowledge, anyway."

George interrupted his closing of the range house and came over to the two of them.

"I can't tell you how sorry I am that this happened. We've never had an incident like this at this club before. We practice strict safety protocols. And, if I had been at the range house when this stranger came in and wanted to shoot his rifle...well, I wouldn't have let him set up at the rifle benches until everybody was off the sporting clays course. I assure you, I'll be bringing this incident up to the monthly board meeting. And what that Wes Smith was up to. Well, maybe the board should review his membership status."

"I've contacted the sheriff's dispatch, George," Andrea informed him. "They'll probably be getting in touch to make some inquiry as to what happened. But it wasn't your fault, and it was probably just a careless discharge."

George's demeanor went from agitated to regretful.

"Well, thanks. But, to have something like this happen on my watch. I feel terrible."

Andrea and Danny shook hands with George and left together into the parking lot.

"I sure hope we're still on for the Mackinaw Brewing Company tonight at 7:00, and that you're still buying," Danny said hopefully with a big grin.

"See you there," Andrea confirmed, answering with that brilliant smile and flashing blue eyes. Danny watched for a moment as she drove off toward Traverse City.

CHAPTER TEN

The hot, mid-afternoon August sun at the gun club had warmed the air and the open grounds of the shotgun ranges. Even the more-shaded woods where the sporting clays course was laid out had become still, hot and sticky with the humidity rising. But then a warm breeze flowed through the woods, generated by a thermal down on the skeet field – a twisting column of hot air rising from the warming ground. For the squad of shooters working their way to the last of the sporting clays stations, even a warm breeze seemed to give some relief to the summer heat and humidity.

The loud crack of a .308 deer rifle had sent a 168-grain, boat tail bullet speeding up the slope from the rifle benches, across the skeet field, straight toward one of the sporting clays shooters standing near the 200-yard backboard for the rifle range, close to the last station for sporting clays. In the split-second in which the bullet traversed the 200 yards, the quickening breeze associated with the thermal caught the bullet ever so slightly, deflecting its flight path to the side by just a couple of inches over that distance.

Instead of striking the human target it had started out for, the bullet whizzed between that person and another standing face-to-face, the two talking to each other. The lead projectile buried itself in the backboard behind them with a dull thud.

The Angel of Providence and Protection kept the thermal rising and twisting over the field below for a few seconds more, the breeze continuing to gust lightly through the trees on the slope, but no second shot followed...and the thermal and its breeze died down. Danny and Andrea were safe and unharmed.

CHAPTER ELEVEN

A few minutes before 4:00, Danny drove up Highway 22 into downtown Suttons Bay and immediately spotted Tiny waiting for him on the sidewalk outside the VI Grill. He was gregariously talking to a family of tourists with a big grin on his face. Seeing Danny's Grand Cherokee pull up to the curb across the street, Tiny said his goodbyes to the tourists and walked over, by now sauntering as though thoroughly enjoying the traffic slowing, and even stopping, for the giant pedestrian.

As soon as he got in and buckled up, Tiny turned to Danny and they both spoke at once.

"You'll never guess what..." Like two little kids, they fumbled around with "You go first...no, you go first..." then started simultaneously again, "I met this woman named...An...gela/drea." Almost giggling like two grade-school boys, they finally settled down and sorted it out, with Tiny telling Danny all about his fascinating coffee date with Angela, and Danny telling Tiny about his shooting sporting clays with Andrea.

"And she's buying me dinner tonight," Tiny added with an ear-to-ear smile. "I'm to meet her back at the store right there at 6:00, although we didn't say where we were going."

"Get outta here," Danny joshed at him. "Andrea and I made plans to meet at the Mackinaw Brewing Company restaurant in Traverse City at 7:00, and, you're not going to believe this, she's buying for me."

The two best friends laughed so hard that the Jeep shook there by the curb. Danny settled down again. "This has to be unheard of in the annals of single, middle-aged men, that we would both meet someone gorgeous and available on the same afternoon in the little area of Leelanau County."

"And that they would both be buying us dinner tonight at their own suggestions," Tiny broke in, still bouncing with laughter.

"Yah, the odds have to be so astronomical that there's no way you could bet on that one," Danny laughed. "Why don't you call Angela right now and suggest that the two of you go with Andrea and me to Mackinaw Brewing. It'll be the most unique double-date of all time, anywhere."

Tiny did so, and the congenial Angela said that'd be great. She'd love to meet Danny and Andrea. Danny, meanwhile, also called Andrea, who was also okay with the idea.

"I remember Angela from going into the shop a time or two," Andrea added, "although it would not have been when I was working, so I wouldn't have been in uniform, and we really didn't talk because she *was* working. But she seemed very friendly and outgoing. I'll be delighted to get further acquainted, and meet your friend Tiny, of course."

The plans set, the two men grinned mightily at each other, indulged in the familiar "fist bump," and Danny pulled away from the curb. They had a couple of hours to dash back to the bed and breakfast, get ready, and then get back to the shop to pick up Angela. But as they drove past the VI Grill on the side street, Danny glanced down the alley and spotted a familiar vehicle parked behind the restaurant.

He stopped abruptly.

CHAPTER TWELVE

Danny could scarcely believe it. Squeezed behind the VI Grill was what had to be Wes Smith's beat-up, rusty, red pickup. Maybe he should have thought first of calling Andrea to tell her, or maybe the sheriff. But he didn't want Wes to come out suddenly, get in his truck, and drive away again, so Danny pulled over and parked alongside the restaurant. He told Tiny that it was the same truck that had roared away from the range house of the gun club.

"Do me a favor and post yourself in the alley here, in case he comes out and tries to drive off before I can talk to him. I'll go in and see if I can spot him. He was a couple of hundred yards off and running top speed the one time I saw him, but I think I can recognize his outfit at least."

"You got it," Tiny agreed. "But give a big holler if things get out of hand in there. Your protection service will come running."

Danny thanked him and entered the side door not far from the alley. It only took a matter of seconds for him to see what had to be Wes Smith sitting at the long bar with a glass of whiskey in his hand, same tattered overalls, scraggly beard.

"You're Wes Smith?" Danny asked him as he stepped up to the bar alongside Smith's stool.

"Yah, and who be you, stranger?" Wes slurred in reply.

"My name is Dan Henriks. I'd like to talk to you for a minute, if I may."

"I guess so, but it'll cost you a whiskey."

Danny motioned to the bartender, "Another round for Mr. Smith, on me."

The bartender raised his eyebrows, but not at the drink order. "Coming right up, but I ain't never heard ol' Wes there called 'Mr. Smith' before," he grinned.

Danny motioned for Smith to slide down a little further to the end of the bar. He wanted to get away from other patrons who were sipping, munching on bar food, and watching the late Sunday afternoon Detroit Tigers game on the overhead television.

Lowering his guard just a bit with the fresh drink in his hand, Wes asked, "So what's this all about stranger?"

"I was on that slope above the skeet range earlier this afternoon when the commotion broke out and saw you run out to the parking lot and pull away in the same red truck that's parked behind this place in the alley."

Wes raised his hands up quickly and leaned away, "Whoa, Nellie. Now hold on there; I wasn't respon...responshible.... for that gunshot."

"Settle down. I don't think you were. But I need to know just what that was all about. Why'd you take off running as soon as the shot rang out and leave in such a hurry?"

"I know my guns," Wes declared. "I knew that it was a rifle shot, that it shouldn't have fired during, during that shotgun shooting time. I figured I better get the hell out of there before someone tried to pin it on me. Folks blame me for all kinds of shit I never done. I wasn't shticking around for someone BS-ing about me," he growled defiantly.

Danny knew he was holding back. "Okay, but that's not the full story. Bill and others in the range house heard you speak up and vouch for some stranger with a bit of a Southern drawl so he could shoot at the rifle range. Just who was he, and what did you have to do with him?"

Wes became more defensive and belligerent. He tilted the glass up and drained the whiskey in one gulp. "I don't think that's any of your damned business. I'm outta here." He slid off the bar stool and strode unsteadily to the door headed out to the alley.

Danny followed him, in the same motion tossing bills on the bar, more than covering the cost of the drink. As soon as he exited through the side door, there was Wes, one arm held behind his back by Tiny. Tiny's other hand pressed Smith's cheek against the door of his truck. Wes undoubtedly felt like protesting and fighting back, but was completely helpless, pinned securely by the much larger man. Clearly terrified, he wasn't even struggling.

"As you can see," Danny said much more firmly, "my friend here also wants to know what you have to say. Now before we call the sheriff, or a worse fate befalls you, tell me what I want to know. Who was this man, and what was your involvement?"

"Okay, okay..." Wes slurred. "Just let go of me, and I'll tell ya."

Tiny eased up and slowly released Smith, glowering at him and at the ready, in case the drunk tried to bolt.

"It, it was, well, like this," Wes started to explain. "I went over to the gun club this afternoon because there's always shome rich guys shooting there on Sundays. I'm a member, and I can get in and shmooze around. I catch 'em arriving in the parking lot, with their fancy guns and shooting stuff, and I offer to help them unload, and, you know, real friendly-like, carry stuff for them over to the range shack. We talk guns and shot shell loads, and at least a few of the regulars will sl-lip a fiver into my hand as, you know, a tip for my being so helpful. That's what paid for my whiskey when you crashed in on me. George and the other officers of the club give me hell if they see me doing that, but, hey, I provide a servish."

"We promise, we won't tell George or anyone else, but you still haven't answered my question," Danny pressed him.

"Oh, yesh." Wes was clearly feeling the effects of the glasses of whiskey more and more, and no longer seemed to care about how much he shared. "Well, I went up to this stranger to offer my help, like with the others. And he shaid that sure, I could carry his gun case and gear bag, but that he'd like my help with shomething else."

"Which was?"

"He smiled and bent over, you know, kinda private-like, and shaid that once his shtuff was on the rifle bench and laid out, he was gonna play a little joke on a friend out on the shporting things course and send a bullet over his head, just to make him jump, you know, scare him a bit. He put a folded-up Franklin in my fist and shaid that all I had to do was vouch for him with George, then hang around by his shtuff, you know, standing so's I was between him and the others. Then, whens I heard the shot, I was to skedaddle out to my truck and take off like a bat outta hell. He didn't say why, but for a C-note, it was fine with me."

"But you don't know who he is or where to find him," Danny asked.

"Never shaw him before. But a real friendly fellow, real nicesh guy."

"Tiny, grab his keys out of the pocket of his overalls."

Tiny grabbed Wes again with one paralyzing grip and he fished the truck keys out of Smith's pocket with his other hand.

"Hey, that'sh my keys," Wes complained.

"Mr. Smith," Danny said sternly, "you're in no condition to drive. Your keys will be left with the bartender, and I'll tell him to make sure that you arrange for alternative transportation. But thanks for your cooperation. That'll be all for now." Danny knew full well that the sheriff deputies would probably be looking up Wes Smith for their own questioning.

Wes instantly relaxed somewhat, however unsteady he appeared, and seemed to feel less threatened, but despite his safe release, he just couldn't leave things alone.

"Don't I at leash get a tip, you know, for being sho helpful?"

"Okay," Danny replied, leaning closer to the inebriated scofflaw, "if I were you, I'd stay away from the Cedar Club for a while...oh, and never, ever, drink and drive drunk."

Danny left Wes looking rather forlornly at his keyless pickup. Tiny and he reentered the VI Grill and informed the bartender of the situation, of Wes being incapable of driving himself home, put the keys on the bar, and went back out to Danny's Jeep.

"Pretty hard to figure out who put that Wes up to that stunt," Tiny stated the obvious.

"Yes," Danny agreed. "But maybe Andrea and the sheriff's department can get a lead. In any case, it sure as hell doesn't qualify for an accidental discharge. And who was the intended target? Andrea? Someone behind us at that last station? Or me? And why?"

CHAPTER THIRTEEN

It was now just an hour and a half until the two friends had to return to the gift shop to pick up Angela, so they headed straight back to the Leelanau Bed & Breakfast to change clothes, run a brush through their hair and otherwise look like they were ready for a dinner date. The three of them would then head down to Traverse City to meet Andrea at the Mackinaw Brewing Company restaurant and bar at 7:00.

Tiny drove the Grand Cherokee, and when they pulled up to the curb outside the gift shop, Danny jumped out and got in the back seat. Precisely at 6:00 Angela came out, while the owner, Sam, locked the door behind her. Tiny greeted her with a big smile on the walk, opened the front passenger-side door for her, and made introductions with Danny in the back. Danny thought to himself that Tiny hadn't exaggerated. Angela was absolutely beautiful, one of most beautiful women he had ever seen.

It was about 6:30 by the time Tiny found a parking place in the jammed-full lot across the Boardman River in downtown Traverse City. The three of them strolled across the wooden foot bridge over the river, chatting and getting further acquainted. Partway across Danny looked over the wooden rail and spotted a large trout holding in a protected pocket among rocks on the stream bottom.

"Wow, look at the size of that baby," he exclaimed. "You two go ahead, I want to watch him for a minute. I'll catch up to you in a jiffy." He figured that would give Tiny and Angela a chance to talk without him butting in like a "third wheel."

Danny watched the big trout finning in the current on the bottom, but also glanced from time to time at the two of them, walking a few steps, stopping to watch the mallard ducks swimming and feeding in the stream. The ducklings of spring had now grown as large as their parents.

Angela and Tiny chuckled together frequently as they talked, she with her pretty laugh and bright, smiling face and Tiny occasionally erupting into his trademark roaring laughter.

Wow, thought Danny, *they really seem to be hitting it off*.

They spent 15-20 minutes of relaxing time by the stream, looking out toward the beautiful water rippling on West Grand Traverse Bay with its many white sails from sailboats tacking back and forth and plumes of spray being kicked up behind the motor boats cruising around. Then the three of them checked in at the hostess's stand in the entrance of the Mackinaw Brewing Company on the corner of Front Street, the main downtown street.

A few minutes later, just before 7:00, Andrea came through the door, and Danny rose from the bench in the waiting area to greet her. She had changed from her shooting clothes earlier in the afternoon into a long, flowing summer dress down to the tops of her sandaled feet. Her blonde hair was down in soft curls, and right away Danny noticed that she had put on a Petoskey stone pendant on a gold chain, with matching Petoskey stone earrings, paired with smaller Leland Blue stone earrings as well.

As they exchanged greetings and a little hug, Tiny nudged Angela sitting next to him and silently mouthed, "Petoskey stones, right?"

Angela leaned closer to him, a fact that Tiny liked a lot, and whispered, "Yes, and Leland Blue earrings, too."

They smiled at each other, and then rose to be introduced to Andrea, who responded with delight at meeting them.

The popular restaurant was bustling and noisy, but their reservation request resulted in their being seated out on the porch, where the warm evening was quieter, despite all the tourist activity going on nearby. Tiny tried the lake perch this time, on his personal mission to sample all the varieties of fish he could during their vacation in Northern Michigan. Then they ordered after-dinner drinks and continued to relax and talk, getting more and more acquainted with each other. After about an hour and a half, Danny wondered to himself if they should vacate their table for other diners. But the dinner traffic had slowed somewhat, and the congenial restaurant staff didn't seem to be hovering as though they wanted the table emptied. So, the four continued to sip and talk. The two women had started acting like old friends in their comfort level with each other.

During a lull in his talking, Danny gazed at Andrea and felt absolutely mesmerized. He had been instantly attracted to her early that afternoon at the gun club, admiring her combination of strength and authority with beauty and intense, blue eyes. And now he was seeing her very feminine side, her beauty expressed in softness and grace. He hadn't been so quickly fascinated with a woman since almost a quarter-century ago when his late wife Samantha had swept him off his feet.

At least a couple of hours passed before they got up and left the table and porch of the restaurant. Both Angela and Andrea had to go to their respective jobs Monday morning, so they needed to start heading home soon, but the four strolled slowly down Front Street, glancing at store front windows and continuing their talking and laughter. It also gave Danny the opportunity to fill Andrea in on the encounter with Wes Smith at the VI Grill.

"That's good to know, what Smith told you," she said. "I'll pass that on to the sheriff's department. Be prepared if they don't like the fact that you were doing your own investigating."

"I know. And I apologize. I didn't mean to interfere with them, or you, but I have to admit that sometimes I'm prone to leap into action rather than leave it to others. I didn't want Wes Smith to slip away without being questioned on what he was doing at the club, and if there was a chance that he could lead them to the man who put him up to it. But I won't stick my nose in any farther, promise."

"Okay, you better not, Buster," she kidded him. Danny was grateful that she didn't seem too mad at his initiative and actions.

They walked Andrea to her Hyundai Santa Fe, but before she got in to drive off, she turned and said to the three of them, "Do you want to do this again later this week? I have Thursday evening open, if that works for you." She added a side comment to Danny, "Church choir rehearsal on Thursdays doesn't resume until next week, but we are singing an old, familiar number this coming Sunday. Wanta come?"

Danny was delighted at her suggestion, and Tiny and Angela glanced at each other, Angela nodding yes, and Tiny boomed out, "And let's try another restaurant. I'll order some different fish, maybe walleye next time." All four laughed.

Tiny and Angela stepped away a bit and talked with each other, while Danny said goodbye to Andrea.

"Do you have some time available earlier in the week when just you and I could get together? If your work permits, of course. Tiny and I are vacationing, so I'm available whenever you want."

Andrea responded with that radiant smile and said, "I'd like that. I have to be on patrol tomorrow, but on Tuesday I have paperwork and reports due before the end of the month and will be at my desk all day, so maybe a lunch break for the two of us, say meet me at the Post at noon?"

"I'll be there, a little before 12:00." Danny took it as a matter of pride that he was almost always punctual. Andrea gave him a warm kiss and a hug, got in her Santa Fe, and left. Danny wondered how he was going to wait until Tuesday noon.

CHAPTER FOURTEEN

Tiny opened the passenger-side door for Angela to get in, and once she had, he turned to Danny, "Hey, man, I hope you won't mind, but Angela's invited me to have a nightcap at her apartment in Suttons Bay. Okay if I drop you off at the bed and breakfast? Oh, and don't wait up," he smiled from ear to ear.

"Moving pretty fast there, brother," Danny kidded him.

"At our age, there's no sense in wasting time. Besides, this woman is the real deal. I don't think I've ever met anyone like her. I just hope she likes me for more than a fast fling."

Danny smiled inwardly. He couldn't remember Tiny ever talking like that about a woman, concerned about what she thinks of *him*, and suggesting hopes for a longer relationship. Most of the time over the years Tiny seemed to regard women as targets for conquest and then move on. What had changed in the big fellow?

"You're making me jealous, buddy, but sure, drop me off. Just remember where to find me tomorrow morning. I'll introduce you to more varieties of fresh-water fish if you get back to me before lunch."

"Have to," Tiny replied, "she still has to be at the shop

before 10:00 when it opens."

Settled back into their room with twin beds at the bed and breakfast, and Tiny having returned to nearby Suttons Bay, Danny sat for a bit in a comfortable wicker chair by the open, screened window. He soaked in the cooling night breeze, the sound of crickets, and the not-far-off hooting of a great horned owl. What a total surprise this day had been, but how great. He probably hadn't been so genuinely at ease and delighted in nearly three years...or more.

Remarkably, even the bullet whizzing by Andrea and him at the gun club didn't traumatize him. It could have. But the dinner with Tiny, Angela, and her that evening had been such a joy. It seemed to overpower the ominous threat of the rifle shot. In any case, he'd wait until tomorrow to give it any further thought, and maybe Andrea and the sheriff's deputies would come up with something. He felt capable of setting it aside.

Tonight was too good not to be savored. If only he could wait until Tuesday noon.

Danny slept soundly, deeply, and without nightmares. The Angel of Providence and Protection never left him.

CHAPTER FIFTEEN

True to his word, Tiny had left Angela's apartment by 9:30, after sweet rolls and coffee at her kitchen table, and drove back to the bed and breakfast. She was able to walk to the shop to start work at 10:00, but not before the two of them made plans for getting together Wednesday evening. He met up with Danny on the back covered patio. Danny had slept in after a truly busy Sunday and enjoyed a late breakfast just before they quit serving at 10:00. He was relaxing with an additional cup of coffee when Tiny sat down.

"Well, Romeo returns," he kidded Tiny, who just smiled as contentedly as he possibly could. "I trust you left Angela without complaints."

Neither Danny nor Tiny were in the habit of bragging in detail about romantic encounters, so Tiny's only reply was to keep smiling.

"She wants to see me again Wednesday evening, so I guess so far, so good."

"Well, I don't get to see Andrea again until Tuesday lunch at noon, so you're moving a lot faster than me, brother. What do you want to do today?"

"I'm going to hit the shower. Then how 'bout driving across the Leelanau Peninsula to that old fishing village at Leland? Didn't you say that that Bluebird Inn has yummy fried smelt on their menu?"

"That they do," Danny confirmed. "I checked their current menu online. Leland it is."

While Tiny showered and shaved, Danny thought late morning might be a time to call and at least check in with Andrea regarding what inquiry was being made into the rifle shot at the gun range yesterday. She answered her cell right away.

"Andrea, it's Danny. Are you okay to talk for just a moment?"

"I am. The sergeant sent me out to monitor traffic this morning, so I'm set up as a dreaded speed trap on Highways 31/37."

"Any success?"

"Monday mornings tend to feature people rushing late to work to start their new week after too much of everything over the weekend, and tourists who decided to stay until Monday morning to stretch out their vacation break and are now tearing back south, also to get to work or whatever. So, yup, I've pulled over eight so far. Was probably too lenient on several more."

"Don't mean to bother you while working," Danny apologized, "but anything happening on yesterday afternoon's rifle shot at the Cedar club?"

"I passed it on to the Leelanau County Sheriff's Department right away yesterday, of course. I checked in with them first thing this morning before coming out here to set up. They'll do everything they can to try to run down who the shooter was, just what he was up to. But as you know, we have amazingly little to go on. Descriptions of this unknown subject didn't give us more than what Bill had told us after it happened.

"And again, nobody saw what became of him, where he went, or any idea what kind of vehicle he was driving. There was nothing distinctive mentioned except maybe a bit of a soft, Southern accent. They *were* going to look up Wes Smith, however, and squeeze him for additional information. They'll get back to me."

"Thanks. I'm just glad you weren't hurt. And sorry to interrupt your work."

"No problem. I wouldn't have answered if I was occupied at the time. Oh, but there's another one, pushing 80 in a 55-mile zone. Later."

***

Danny and Tiny made it across the peninsula to the Bluebird Inn for lunch. It wasn't far, and the drive over rolling hills, past farms and vineyards and wineries and forested areas, was beautiful and relaxing. The summer season was showing ripening and maturity, with orchards full of peaches about to be picked and apples soon to be ready for harvest. Fields of hay and grain already being reaped. As advertised, Tiny had a basket of crispy, fried smelt, then ordered another one. Danny had the broiled whitefish fillet for which the Bluebird was famous.

Their afternoon consisted of more touring of the Leelanau Peninsula, culminating in the boardwalk and overlook at Sleeping Bear Point. A few years previous that spot had been voted "Most Beautiful Place in America" in a *Good Morning America* television poll, and it was easy to see why. The combination of great sand dunes towering 400 feet and more above the soothing water of Lake Michigan, the lowering sun sparkling off the ripples below, a lake freighter cruising by offshore, the giant trees, the legendary Sleeping

Bear Dune itself, with the Manitou Islands out in the big lake...it made more than one viewer describe the whole scene as breathtaking. A woman standing nearby shared that it was her happy place.

Danny and Tiny agreed that they would eat supper in at the Leelanau Bed & Breakfast and spend a quiet evening kicking back there. Danny had stopped at the Empire Inn and picked up a personal-size pepperoni pizza to go; Tiny had taken out a third basket of smelt, paying for extra smelt, from the Bluebird Inn. Danny was about convinced that Tiny would soon be sprouting fins and gills...and that his swimming would greatly improve, despite his great bulk.

Danny was really looking forward to tomorrow's lunch with Andrea, and Tiny was looking for a way to skip Tuesday entirely and get right to Wednesday evening back with Angela. They did not give a thought or word to the man who left the state that day with his rifle hidden in the back of his vehicle.

CHAPTER SIXTEEN

Tuesday Danny dropped Tiny off for a lunch on his own in downtown Suttons Bay and met Andrea at the State Police Post on 14th Street in Traverse City just a few minutes before noon. She had only about 45 minutes of lunch break available, so they dashed down to the Grand Traverse Pie Company, where food and service was quick. They picked up their already-prepared orders at the end of the counter. The day was warm and sunny, so they sat at an outside table.

"Mm-m, this Quiche Lorraine is good," Andrea smiled and licked her lips. Danny noticed how she again pulled off looking both authoritative and professional in her state police uniform, her blonde hair gathered back tightly, and yet beautiful and feminine at the same time. She had greeted him at the Post with some appropriate reserve, but as soon as they were out the door, seemed virtually to bubble with enthusiasm at being with him. *Remarkable*, he thought.

"I don't have anything more about that unknown subject who fired the shot at the range Sunday afternoon," she went on. "It's in the sheriff department's hands now, and while they can communicate with me out of courtesy, with so little to go on we probably can't expect it to be a high priority for them. I have no idea if they've tracked down Wes Smith yet. He's probably lying pretty low, waiting for them to lose interest. But when they do talk to him, from what you said it doesn't sound like he has much to offer."

"That's okay," Danny replied. "My primary concern is that there's not someone out there who might want to take another potshot at you, for whatever reason."

Andrea wrinkled her brow at that thought. "I really can't imagine that. Even Wes Smith can't be a personal threat to me. Sure, I've pulled him over at least a couple of times for speeding and DUI, but he's actually been congenial about that, admitting that he was in the wrong. Of course, lots of people do that, hoping that I'll let them off with a warning, or go easy on their ticket," she laughed.

"But let's change the subject. I'm buried in that paperwork and reports for all of today. Sarge has been on my back about letting that stuff pile up in my in-basket. And I won't be worth the company this evening, but how about drinks and snacks tomorrow evening? I'll be back on patrol for my Wednesday shift, assuming I'm not put on administrative leave for not finishing my reports." The two of them laughed, and Andrea continued, "Should be easy duty. You up for getting together about 7:00 again?"

"And just the two of us this time," Danny wanted that to be clear. "Angela and Tiny have their own plans that evening."

"Perfect. Now I have to get back, I'm afraid. Sarge didn't even want me to leave for my lunch break, but I told him it was case-related," she winked.

Danny loved seeing that wink and radiant smile.

After dropping Andrea off at the Post, Danny, ever the theologian, thought about Andrea's use of the word "perfect." He just couldn't help thinking that nothing, nothing at all, this side of the kingdom of heaven was Perfect. All on earth and in the great, enveloping cosmos was fallible and imperfect. Add to that the all-too-common habit these days for some folks to toss in "perfect" as virtually a throw-away exclamation. The server in a restaurant takes his order and clicks her pen shut with a smiling "perfect." *How did the concept of Absolute Perfection turn into such triviality?* he wondered. But that didn't apply to Andrea just now. The way she said it, it was obvious to him that she meant it, as though she couldn't conceive of anything better than the two of them getting together tomorrow night, at least he hoped that was how she felt.

He met up with Tiny again in the downtown park in Suttons Bay, watching the parents and their children play and the local ducks paddling around. Tiny had dropped by the gift shop, of course, and flirted and chuckled with Angela when she wasn't busy, while she flirted back and giggled. If for no other reason than to keep her engaged with him, he picked out and bought a Petoskey stone watch band and a Leland Blue stone pendant on an 18-carat gold chain. He was wearing both already, along with his perpetual, many times repaired, friendship bracelet from New Life Community Church. He also sported a constant smile.

What a change, Danny thought, *from a feared street gang leader in the African-American slum district of the Hill back in Pittsburgh, to a sometimes sullen, even ominous, "businessman" ordering his "boys" around in activities from legal to highly illegal, to now a mellow, laid-back giant who seemed as smitten as an adolescent boy who had just discovered girls, or more accurately, perhaps The Girl/Love of His Life.*

They explored more of the Leelanau Peninsula that afternoon, playing tourist, including several of the Natural Areas that had been bought and preserved by the Leelanau Conservancy.

They turned in early at the bed and breakfast to be able to get up and out first thing Wednesday morning. On their way out at 6:00 a.m., they grabbed sacks of "breakfast to go" that were thoughtfully prepared for them by the cook. Tiny's was especially full, as the cook had quickly learned about his prodigious appetite.

Their plan and itinerary for the day included the 120 miles to Mackinaw City, the famous fudge and gift shops, especially the fudge, and the "Mighty Mac" Bridge, arguably the most graceful suspension bridge in the world. And enhanced by an almost-wilderness setting around it. With about two-and-a-half hours' drive each way, the two best friends gave up on their original plan to spend a full afternoon and into the evening on picturesque Mackinac Island. It had become of supreme importance to both of them to get back to Traverse City and Suttons Bay before 6:00. Angela and Andrea would be waiting.

It turned out to be a fun day for both Tiny and Danny, but if they had been forthcoming about it, each of them was considerably pre-occupied. Love, if that was what this truly was, has a way of doing that. The Angel continued to Protect and was Providing beyond their greatest expectation.

CHAPTER SEVENTEEN

Danny dropped Tiny off at Angela's apartment in Suttons Bay about 6:30. She had gotten off work at the shop at 6:00 and had invited Tiny to her place for dinner. They planned to spend a quiet, relaxing evening together, and Tiny would call Danny on his cell if there was any reason, however unlikely, that he needed a ride before the next morning.

Danny had just enough time to make it down to Traverse City, where he met Andrea at her condo. She came down right away when he called to let her know that he had arrived. The weather was still warm on this last Wednesday in August, and she had changed out of her uniform into shorts, sandals, and a lacy cotton blouse that was pleasingly form-fitting. She had again let her hair down into soft waves, which Danny thought made her look even more gorgeous. Her smiling greeting was enthusiastic, and they hugged and exchanged a light kiss. Danny really liked the way things seemed to be going.

"Let's drive downtown, park across the river, and walk over to Front Street," Andrea suggested. "You like pizza? It's really good at Pangea."

"Sounds good to me," Danny agreed. "Tiny and I have been eating so much great fish, a change of pace will do me good."

Andrea obviously wasn't shy, had a take-charge personality, but wasn't overbearing or offensive about it. In a way it reminded him of Sarah, who was an early love in their days together at the University of Pittsburgh, but Sarah was genuinely used to getting her own way on almost everything, and he didn't sense that about Andrea...just that she was a strong woman who had no problem taking the initiative. It was a trait he found very appealing.

After splitting a medium-size pizza, they strolled along Front Street again, then crossed the same foot bridge over the Boardman River and went under the East Grandview Parkway by means of the underground pedestrian tunnel. They made their way to the Open Space along the shore of West Grand Traverse Bay, found a bench and sat down to look out at the water. There were swimmers at the beach, and the usual abundance of sail and motor boats, including several fishermen in boats clustered near the mouth of the river as it flows into the bay. The water was only lightly rippled in the soft breeze and reflected an amazingly beautiful range of colors of blue.

Danny was overcome by a feeling beyond continued healing. It was also a peace and contentment the likes of which he had never fully experienced before. With Andrea at his side, the two of them continually talking and learning more about each other, this feeling was growing.

"You said when we were together with Angela and Tiny that he and you are here just for this week?" she asked.

"I'm afraid so, Andrea. We have to drive back to Pittsburgh on Sunday. I'd like to attend your church that morning. It would be great to hear you and your choir. Do you suppose we could have a brunch together right after your worship service, and then Tiny and I would hit the road for Pennsylvania?"

"Sounds good to me. But first, why don't we walk to your Jeep, drive back to my condo, and you come up for a bit of Crown Royal Black?"

Danny smiled with pleasure. Not only had Andrea noted his favorite brand of Canadian whiskey, but he hoped fervently that she had more in mind than a sip of whiskey. She did, and Tiny and Danny had very satisfying conclusions to their evenings. Well aware that Andrea had to report at the state police post early Thursday morning, Danny exited Andrea's condo a little before 11:00, but she sent him on his way with a long, passionate kiss and a very tight embrace.

"Shall I pick you up again tomorrow evening for our dinner date with Angela and Tiny?" he asked.

"Sure, I'd like that. Truth is, I'll be doing a lot of driving again tomorrow on patrol, so I'm glad to have someone else behind the wheel. But why don't you have Tiny drive, and you and I take the back seat? It can be *very* cozy," she winked and flashed that fabulous smile.

"Great idea," Danny agreed. As he went down the stairs and out the building's door, he sported a very big smile himself and again appreciated how Andrea didn't hesitate to take the initiative. This was easily the best vacation he had ever had.

CHAPTER EIGHTEEN

Danny left the bed and breakfast the next morning in time to pick Tiny up outside Angela's apartment at 9:30, while she got ready to walk to the shop. Tiny had wanted to take the day to drive up to the Hartwick Pines State Park outside Grayling, Michigan, to see the towering white and red pines there. It was unique acreage, some of the only "virgin" pine trees not to have been cut down during the 19th century logging days in the state.

As they walked through the magnificent stand of pines – some of the trees reaching up 170-175 feet or even more – the winding path eventually brought them to the picturesque log chapel that had been built on a small hill among the big trees. They entered and sat down on one of the small pew benches, just being quiet and listening to the wind outside *whooshing* through the pine boughs high above. It was marvelously peaceful, and it was hard not to feel particularly reverent and close to the Creator.

Finally, Tiny broke the welcome silence, but practically whispered as he did so.

"Danny, I have to tell you, not only has this been the vacation of a lifetime for me, but I also believe I've fallen in love. Angela is gorgeous, smart, funny, good-hearted, and best of all, I think she really likes me for the man I am. More than that, she makes me want to be better than the man I am, for her. I've never met anyone like her, and I don't want to even think about looking for another." Tiny leaned back and smiled as broadly as he could, which was a *really* big smile.

Danny adopted a cautionary tone.

"You know, my friend, it's only been four days since you first met her. I've never known you to be a 'love at first sight' kinda guy. You sure?"

"Never been surer of anything in my life. I'm thinking of selling my businesses in Pittsburgh, looking into that idea of providing security products and services up here in Northern Michigan, but first asking that woman to be my wife. But I don't want her to feel too rushed into anything," he hastened to add.

"Well, I don't blame you," Danny shifted his tone to be more supportive. "She *is* terrific. Almost as beautiful and sensational as Andrea," he kidded the big guy with a light punch to his massive shoulder. "But you have heard about the amount of cold and snow they get up here, haven't you? It's not like our winters in Pittsburgh."

"In case you haven't noticed, bro', I'm well-insulated for the cold. Besides, if she feels about me the way I feel about her, our love can keep us warm," Tiny smiled. "I'm serious, though, I think I could make the move, especially for her. She loves it up here."

Danny paused for a second, and then made his own admission. "Well, I don't want to assume too much too soon when it comes to Andrea, but in the last few days I've felt deeply for someone for the first time since my late wife Samantha passed on. I sure want to see what can come of this relationship. It damn well feels like real love."

"Come on then," Tiny insisted. "Let's get back to Suttons Bay and go meet those ladies for tonight's supper out. Love is in the air-r-r," he sang in his deep bass. Their pace picked up as they trod the path back to the Hartwick Pines parking lot. The surrounding big trees were still majestic, but the focus and talk of the two best friends was on the two women waiting for them that evening.

CHAPTER NINETEEN

The four-way conversation over dinner at the Tuscan Bistro on Highway 22 was filled with laughs and fun, as they continued to get to know each other more fully. By this time Angela and Andrea were sharing and acting like long-time friends who greatly enjoyed each other's company, as well as the company of their men.

Tiny spoke up and asked Angela, "Danny and I are going to see more of this beautiful area the next couple of days, but he suggested that me and him go to worship at Andrea's Presbyterian Church in Traverse City Sunday morning before we drive back to Pittsburgh that afternoon and evening. Do you want to attend with us and the four of us go out for a pancake brunch after?"

"Way ahead of you, big boy," Angela grinned and kidded him. "Andrea already asked me, and I said, sure, I'd love to worship with the three of you and hear her and her choir."

"We'll be glad to pick you up again at your apartment that morning, and take you back after brunch," Danny offered.

Tiny and Angela looked just a little bit sheepishly at each other, and Tiny corrected Danny slightly, "Ah, actually you'll be picking up both of us."

"Oh, sure," he smiled a bit awkwardly, and the other three laughed at his hint of embarrassment.

Andrea moved the conversation forward by asking with definite seriousness, "I don't think that Angela will mind if I speak for both of us. What are your plans at this point? Do the two of you intend to return here soon? We hope so."

"Tiny and I both need to get back to Pittsburgh Sunday night, albeit late. Our schedules are light for Monday. I actually don't need to be back in my church office until Tuesday morning, but have some things I have to do Monday. That evening I'm meeting with Tim Murphy, my Associate Pastor, and his partner, Mark, for their wedding planning. Their wedding on the Saturday after Labor Day will be the first same-sex marriage service ever held at South Presbyterian Church."

"That's great," Andrea said, with Angela nodding in the affirmative.

Angela spoke up, "I didn't know your Presbyterian churches allowed that."

Andrea responded quickly, "It's a fairly recent development. Oh, but I should let the Rev. Dr. Daniel speak to that...." and she made a cheerful motion of handing off to Danny the explanation.

"Andrea's right," he affirmed. "In a recent, national meeting of the Presbyterian Church's General Assembly, with voting representatives from all over the country, Presbyterian pastors were given discretion to conduct same-sex marriage ceremonies in states where the practice is legal. They're even working on changing the official definition of marriage from 'a woman and a man' to 'two people.' Tim and Mark have been domestic partners for several years. At last they rejoice that they can become spouses to each other and be married in the eyes of both church and state."

"If you don't mind my asking," Angela resumed, "how has

your congregation responded to having a gay pastor serving them? Has there been conflict or dissension?"

"I'm afraid so," Danny admitted. "Some church members left when they found out about Tim's homosexuality, thinking that it was an offense to God when it was actually offensive to their bigoted thinking. After all, God created him as he is. Some members have been unhappy with Tim only for reasons of his private life, but have stayed, choosing just not to interact with him much. But the worst negativity has been on the part of the 'PUP's'."

"PUP's?" Andrea laughed as Angela also snickered. "What would puppies have to do with it?"

Tiny jumped in, chortling also, "Danny told me about those folks. The acronym stands for 'Presbyterians United for Purity.' Isn't that right, Danny?"

"Exactly right," Danny affirmed. "A group of pastors and lay people from various Presbyterian churches in Pennsylvania and neighboring Ohio got together a number of years ago to 'organize.' They oppose not only the created fact of homosexuality but also a number of other things that they believe taint the 'Purity' of their own concepts of Christianity, the Church, the Bible, and especially their bigotry.

"They've made fusses at a variety of Presbyterian Church meetings and events. They sometimes hold public rallies and picket churches with their crude placards and have even engaged in 'egging' cars of Presbyterian pastors and others, scratching paint on car doors, and other acts of vandalism. Like all of us, they have a right to their own, privately-held beliefs, and even the right and freedom to speak out publicly about those ideas, but some of them can be downright nasty and threaten even worse violence. So far none of them have fire-bombed a church or committed murder, but a few times their disorganized 'protests' have resulted in at least minor assaults on innocent people."

Angela reacted with genuine horror on her face, "That's awful. How do people like that call themselves 'Christian?'"

"Yeah," Andrea agreed. "If they have so much concern about the 'purity' of their Holy Bibles, where in the New Testament does it talk about Jesus hating people, assaulting them, or throwing eggs? After all, didn't he say, 'Let the one who is without sin cast the first...' Well, okay, that was 'stone,' but I feel pretty sure it would apply to eggs," she laughed.

"From the way they speak, write, and act," Danny explained further, "whether they themselves are without sin or not doesn't seem to concern them. Their focus is on what they perceive as the sins of others."

Angela was still upset and continued, "Well, I'm no Bible scholar, but I remember from growing up in my Baptist church in South Central LA that Jesus was very strict about not judging others for their private lives, 'lest ye be judged' by God for trying to take over the divine right of Judgment. Who could Tim and his partner Mark be hurting in their love for each other? What they do in the privacy of their own lives and home is their right and business, just like it is for any of us, including those PUP people. Betcha not all of them are so 'pure' and righteous."

Danny chuckled and admitted, "I do know of at least one of them — a colleague who shall remain anonymous, of course — who has engaged in adultery on more than one occasion, including in a hotel while the national General Assembly meeting was going on. So, no one's perfect, no, not one, and...."

Tiny interrupted, "Damn straight, Danny...oh, sorry, ladies...," but Andrea and Angela just snickered, so he went on, "but tell 'em, Danny, about the whole 'puppies' thing," he chortled.

"I try always to respect everyone else's right to their

beliefs and their free speech," Danny responded, "so let the record show among us four that this doesn't apply to my own behavior. But when this disorganized group 'organized,' they were very proud of the name they chose for their protest movement: Presbyterians United for Purity. They put it on letterhead stationery, their placards, press releases, all kinds of stuff."

Tiny was finding it difficult to contain himself. He felt like Danny was taking too long to get to the point, which everyone who knew Danny very well knew was his tendency, so he jumped in again.

"And the dim bulbs heading up their disorganization apparently didn't stop to think about how their acronym was going to come across to others, you know, that they were just a bunch of little 'puppies' making noise and not knowing how to behave properly."

Danny didn't mind a bit being interrupted, but he picked up his explanation where he left off. "It all got kind of funny, actually. These folks would show up in a small group at a Presbytery meeting, or in front of a church they thought deserved to be picketed because of their welcoming of anyone to their services and activities, whether straight, gay, lesbian, bisexual, transgender, or questioning. And someone in the crowd would say, "Hey, there's those puppy people.'"

"Serves them right I'd say," Angela declared.

"Maybe so," Danny chuckled, "but it just made the PUP's circle their wagons of presumed purity even tighter. Some of their 'camp followers' and lesser-committed members couldn't take their self-imposed embarrassment and drifted away. That left the more hardcore folks to look in on themselves and their self-righteousness as the militant true believers. We have a couple of those fellows who still come to our church. Their wives tag along with their 'cause,' but are probably much less committed."

"The trouble-making husbands mingle and grumble and agitate however they can. Occasionally they concoct some stunt like introducing a resolution at a congregational meeting that our members vote to condemn homosexuality as a sin against God and thereby protect marriage and humanity in general. They never succeed. They've even brought one or two of their placards to worship services or events."

"Wait a minute," Angela reacted; "okay, I understand that those folks may interpret the Bible in their own way, and have their own beliefs against homosexuality, however much some of them may indulge in adultery or promiscuity, but that doesn't make sense. How does someone else's straightness, gayness, private life in their own home, even if they are adulterous or promiscuous, how does that threaten *my* sexuality, my private life, or the sacred institution of marriage?"

"Yeah," Andrea joined in, "Angela and I have both been married in the past – you, too, Danny. Have our marriages, our private lives, our individual sexualities, ever been destroyed, harmed, or threatened in any way by what someone else was doing in their union, their private life, their own sexuality? I agree, the whole mess doesn't make sense at all. First off, it's between God, your spouse, your partner, and you. Nobody else's business."

Danny smiled and once more liked the strength and decisiveness of this beautiful woman.

Tiny made the mood somewhat lighter again. "Well, nobody's going to appoint themselves the 'bedroom police' for this black boy. I can always plead 'discrimination.'" The four erupted in laughter, causing a few people at nearby tables to turn and smile. Tiny continued, "And if anyone would assume that they need to poke themselves into *my* sex life, or tell me what to do, it sure as hell isn't going to be any

PUPPY."

Angela reflexively responded with, "Don't you worry, Sugar, you don't need *anyone* to tell you what or how to...." and then caught herself with a bit of a blush and awkward smile. They all laughed even more.

"Ah, but I never got around to answering all of your initial questions, Andrea," Danny said. "Tiny and I have talked while we were driving around this northern forest, and we both agreed that there couldn't be any more beautiful time to be here than in the fall color season. Even now some of the weaker trees and branches are hinting at the approaching autumn with splashes of red and orange. I have two more weeks of vacation coming to me this year."

"And I can get back to Pittsburgh, attend to my business interests there, but get away again in a few weeks," Tiny added.

"So," Danny continued, "would the two of you be open to a couple of Pennsylvania boys coming back here in about a month, say for the first week of October?"

Angela beamed and leaned over to hug Tiny. Andrea adopted a more serious look, however, and replied, "I don't know now. Which Pennsylvania boys might that be? It better not be those two PUPs," she scowled.

They all roared and couldn't help themselves; the restaurant resounded briefly with their laughter. Nearby patrons and the entire restaurant staff, even those out in the kitchen, looked with a combination of amusement and wonder at what those four were doing now.

It was a great night for Tiny and Danny and proceeded to get even greater. This time Danny sent Tiny on his way in the Grand Cherokee to go back to Angela's apartment. Andrea had invited Danny to spend the night at her place. Tiny was settling in just fine in Angela's apartment. Neither cared a rat's ass about the cost of the empty room at the bed and breakfast. And Danny didn't care much how long it took for Tiny to get back down to Traverse City Friday morning. Andrea had to get up and report in at the Post for work that day, but she graciously suggested that Danny could make himself at home and leave whenever Tiny came to pick him up. The passion and love that night was intense and satisfying for all four of them, and there was no adultery involved, nor, for that matter, any promiscuity, since none of them was in an intimate relationship with anyone else...not that it was anyone else's business.

CHAPTER TWENTY

Andrea had to conduct night patrol Friday night, with all the typical tourist and weekender traffic on the state highways, and Angela had to work late at the gift shop with its later hours on Fridays and Saturdays, so Danny and Tiny spent Friday in the Traverse City area and Friday night back at the bed and breakfast. They both checked in with their loves, however, and all four looked forward to being together again on Saturday morning.

Danny and Tiny picked Angela up at her apartment. The three drove down to Traverse City and likewise picked Andrea up at her condo, and they all went to the terrific Farmers Market that was set up in the parking lot across the Boardman River from downtown. It was the last Saturday in August by now, and the booths and tables were full of fresh produce, a great deal of it advertised as organic, all-natural, from small family farms and gardens. In addition to all the fresh fruits and vegetables, there were booths with hand-crafted, artisan soaps and oils, freshly-picked bunches of flowers, organic beef and pork, some jewelry and other craft items for sale, and an Odawa family selling their freshly-caught lake trout and whitefish.

Tiny took particular interest in the lake trout, realizing that it was one variety of fish he had missed sampling in all the eating out they had done, so Angela offered to broil one for him that evening if he wanted to buy it.

"It's really good, especially just caught early this morning. You'll like it, Sugar."

Tiny visibly licked his lips, "Sounds great. Do you have a charcoal grill? We could barbeque it. But it's more than the two of us can eat, even with my big appetite. Where do you suppose we could find someone to share it with?" He looked over the milling crowd in the Farmers Market, easy to do with his height, as though searching for dinner companions.

"Hey," Danny made mock protest, "we're right here, you know. And I thought we were friends."

"Of course, you're invited," Angela flashed her radiant smile. "Don't pay big boy no mind. He's all bark. But he's definitely not a 'pup.'" And the four couldn't resist a good laugh.

Some vacationers coming down the walkway between booths heard and saw them, assumed they were delighting in the marvelous fresh fish, and immediately stepped up to look and buy. The four moved on, and Angela and Andrea bought a variety of produce for their own kitchens for the coming week. It was a fun morning, colorful, soon to be delicious, and topped off with cappuccinos and lattes at Morsels over on Front Street.

Angela had to be at the shop to work the afternoon and evening, while Andrea had the weekend off, so the four drove up to Suttons Bay and delivered Angela to her work. Then the three parked across the street and went into the 45th Parallel Café for sandwiches for lunch. Tiny got a ham and cheese to go for Angela and hustled back across Highway 22 to deliver it to her.

While he was gone, Andrea smiled and said to Danny,

"You have a great friend there, and he seems very much in love with Angela, who's obviously wonderful herself. The four of us have so much fun when we're together."

"Yeah, he really is. I couldn't ask for a better, more faithful friend," Danny agreed. "He saved my life, maybe more than once, and like they say, he's always there for me, always has my back. You ever read what C. S. Lewis wrote in his *The Four Loves* – about the love of true friends?"

"I have. That *philea*, the love of true friends, is second only to the pure and perfect love of God."

"Right," Danny confirmed, "*agape*, God's love, the total surrender of self in love of the other."

"I really love it that the two of you have made plans to be back up here for the first week of October," Andrea took his hand and gave it a loving caress and squeeze. The warmth and emphasis that she put into saying "really love it" was not lost on Danny.

When Tiny got back to the two of them after delivering lunch to Angela, they sat, ate, sipped and talked for a while. Danny dropped Tiny off at the bed and breakfast, where he declared that he was going to take a nap after a lot of late-night activity that week. Then Danny agreed to drive Andrea back to Traverse City since she declared that she just had to do some wash after a busy week.

"You must have a pile of dirty laundry. If you want to grab it, I can toss it in with mine and I'll give it back to you this evening," she offered.

Maybe this really is serious, Danny chuckled to himself, *if she's willing to do laundry for me*. He thanked her profusely, drove her back to Traverse City, and dropped her and his laundry off at her condo. To save him from more shuttling back and forth, Andrea suggested that she would drive herself up to Angela's for their late fish dinner that evening.

By the time Angela left the closed-up shop, Danny, Tiny, and Andrea converged on Angela's apartment and all set about helping with the preparation of their lake trout with the fresh vegetables purchased that morning. The fillets were carefully broiled over charcoal, sprinkled with lemon juice and herbs, and the zucchini, onions, green peppers and big mushrooms were skewered shish-kebob style and cooked over charcoal, while periodically basted with a butter and herb mixture. At the conclusion of their feast, the four sat on Angela's deck, enjoying the gathering twilight on a soft evening, and agreed enthusiastically that none of their restaurant dining that week could surpass the meal they had just put together themselves.

Tiny stayed for the night at Angela's apartment as planned. Danny and Andrea agreed that he would drive back to the bed and breakfast, finish packing and gathering up stuff for both himself and Tiny and get ready for their road trip back to Pittsburgh the next day after church and brunch. Tiny had done most of his packing when there for his nap. Andrea wanted to go over her music back at her condo, including a solo part she had for tomorrow's service, but she had more in mind for that evening.

"I'm afraid I didn't bring your clean clothes with me when I drove up here for supper," Andrea fake-apologized. "They're still in the dryer. You'll have to come down and get them," she teased. "Say about 10:00?" she breathed with the deadliest *come-hither* look Danny had ever received. His vaunted punctuality would not be in jeopardy that evening.

CHAPTER TWENTY-ONE

Danny returned to the bed and breakfast late Saturday night. He slept completely relaxed. Fortunately, Sunday morning all was pretty much packed and ready to be loaded, including the clean laundry, except for his toiletries and Saturday's clothes he changed out of. He put everything in the back of the Grand Cherokee, swung around to Angela's apartment in Suttons Bay and picked up Tiny and her by 9:00 to go to church.

"I only did the bed part at Leelanau Bed & Breakfast last night since I knew we would be going to brunch this morning," Danny explained as the two of them got in the back seats. "But the hostess was very nice about letting me stuff a to-go bag with Danishes and doughnuts. Help yourselves."

"That's my man," Tiny beamed, grabbing the bag. He should have held it open to Angela first, but couldn't help himself and looked down into the sweet contents. "Yum, Slick would be ecstatic if he was here." Slick had been Tiny's second-in-command for years in Tiny's business ventures in Pittsburgh. He had been known to have raided trash cans for still-fresh doughnuts, he loved them so.

Tiny quickly caught himself, however, and offered the bag to Angela, who indulged in an apricot Danish with a delighted smile and a thank you. The sweets called for a cup of coffee, so they got four cups to go at the nearby 45th Parallel Café, one of them for Andrea, of course. Danny warned Tiny to be sure to save her at least one of the Danishes.

Andrea had gone to the church early for pre-worship choir rehearsal, so the plan was to meet her there. The four huddled briefly in the narthex, Andrea in her choir robe, before the service at 10:00, and they all hugged and laughed and said how each was looking forward to their brunch afterward. Several the church members milling around in the narthex stopped to greet and welcome them, shaking hands and making introductions. Andrea went back to rejoin her fellow choir members. Angela politely excused herself to use the restroom after the roll and coffee.

"I did it, man," Tiny erupted to Danny as soon as she had left. "Last night I asked Angela if she would marry me. I even got down on one of my football-injured knees and said, 'Please marry me and make me the happiest man on earth.'"

"And?" Danny urged him on.

"She said 'yes.' Whatta think she said?" Tiny whacked him on the arm with one of his huge hands. "We were going to tell the two of you at brunch, but I just couldn't wait to tell you. But don't let on to Andrea just yet. I think Angie wants to be there when she's told."

"Well, that'll be a first. Will 'Tiny' Jones walking down the aisle to get hitched. You better have me officiate and tie the knot properly, or I'll be the one to do the whacking," Danny growled at him. "You two have a date, a place, any details?"

"Nah, we were, well, a little too busy last night to get all that gone over. But she's going to take time off for a long weekend this coming Friday through Monday and come to

Pittsburgh to be with me. I said I would buy her ticket, first-class like she deserves, and get her, okay, us, a suite at the downtown Hilton. So long as it's okay with Tim and his partner Mark, we'll attend their wedding next Saturday, maybe take notes, talk with you about our marriage service, get it all worked out."

"Wow, this was fast," Danny responded, on the one hand not surprised, but on the other hand, blown away. "Have you talked about your life together? Were you serious about selling your businesses, pulling up roots there in the Hill, and moving your bulk to the North Woods?"

"Dead serious. Nope, more accurate to say for the first time ever, Truly Alive Serious. Sure, there's a lot to work out, but you know my Nana passed on years ago. I never had any kids. Other than a couple of distant cousins, no family back there. Slick, Speed, and my other 'boys' really run our operations by now, so they'll be glad to buy me out and keep all the profits for themselves. It's time to retire and create something great here in Northern Michigan, beginning with love and happiness with Angela. Oh, but here she comes, so mum's the word for now."

While both Tiny and Danny were considerably preoccupied with the excitement of Tiny's news, the worship service was inspiring and very well done. The pastor's sermon was well-crafted, on the theme of *God's Spiritual Gifts*, based on the New Testament Letter of Paul to the Romans, chapter 12. Among other parts, the scripture "Let love be genuine; hate what is evil, hold fast to what is good; love one another with mutual affection... rejoice in hope..." spoke loudly and clearly to both of them.

The choir anthem was a simple but tasteful arrangement of the old Shaker classic hymn, *Simple Gifts*, and Andrea's solo part rang out through the sanctuary in her fine second soprano:

"And when we find ourselves in the place just right,
'Twill be in the valley of love and delight."

The choir director turned at the conclusion of the brief hymn and led the entire congregation in repeating the song, including, "'twill be in the valley of love and delight." Angela's Baptist soprano voice joined in and soared in what felt like a heavenly chorus, and Tiny and Danny truly felt the love and delight.

They left as quickly as they could after the service, but not before several people encouraged them to be sure to come back, and that Angela should join the choir. They went to The Omelette Shop in Traverse City for pancakes and eggs. Danny rode with Andrea in her Santa Fe and Tiny drove Angela in the Jeep. As soon as they were settled in a booth and had ordered beverages, Angela and Tiny shared their engagement news.

"That's wonderful," Andrea rejoiced. "I'm so happy for both of you. We are, that is," and she smiled happily at Danny.

Danny liked it that Andrea spoke for them as a couple.

"We are, very happy," he agreed. He looked at Andrea and thought how he'd like for the two of them to make such an announcement one of these days. Maybe when Tiny and he came back to Northern Michigan for the first week of October the time would be right.

In the parking lot the four of them exchanged hugs and kisses and the warmest of goodbyes, that they would be all together again in a few weeks, safe traveling. Danny walked Andrea to her car, while Tiny and Angela went to the Jeep to wait for him. Tiny and Danny would drive Angela back up to Suttons Bay, drop her off at her apartment, then turn back south to start heading for Pittsburgh.

Danny and Andrea exchanged another embrace and kiss at her car. He looked into those sparkling blue eyes he adored so much.

"I can hardly wait until the big guy and I are back in October," Danny said to her. "Maybe you and I could have something to announce ourselves." He smiled and winked, dropping the biggest hint he had ever uttered in his life.

Much to his surprise, Andrea stepped back just a bit, squared her shoulders in that ramrod, professional law enforcement stance that expressed authority and control, and said, "There's something I haven't told you, Daniel. At the end of this week my lieutenant came to me and said that there was a position that had opened up downstate at the 6th District Headquarters in Grand Rapids. It would be a promotion for me, with a pay raise, of course, and would advance my career. I haven't given him my answer yet."

Feeling rather stunned at this change of course, Danny stuttered a reply.

"Ah, well, congratulations on such an opportunity. But I guess...that is, I thought you loved it here...that it's home...and, well, what about our return trip in October?" His mind whirled with a feeling of confusion.

Andrea spoke with a power and intensity that he hadn't really heard since she had ordered the men on the sporting clays course last Sunday to get down and stay down after the rifle shot.

"Having you come back here in October means more to me than anything," She looked him squarely in the eye, "but I'm not sticking around here for a 'maybe.'"

If the Angel of Providence and Protection had assumed corporeal form, it would have swatted Danny across the back of his thick head. As it was, the poor sap acted like a light bulb had just lit up above his head. What was he waiting for?

"Well, then, Andrea Wilkins, will you marry me?"

"Yes, of course I'll marry you. What took you so long?"

They closed into another tight embrace and even longer,

more passionate kiss, and then rushed back to the Jeep to tell Angela and Tiny. It would be a double wedding and Danny would not, despite his prior insistence, be available to officiate for Tiny and Angela. He would be standing alongside them.

CHAPTER TWENTY-TWO

On the drive back to Pittsburgh, Danny and Tiny talked of little else but their amazing engagements to what had to be the world's two most wonderful women. In their hurried goodbyes in the restaurant parking lot, Danny and Andrea agreed that they would talk a lot over the phone about their wedding date and all the details. But Andrea was already delighted with the suggestion that they make it a double ceremony with Angela and Tiny. Tiny, meanwhile, would be flying Angela into Pittsburgh on Friday next to join him for Tim and Mark's wedding at South Presbyterian Church. A long weekend would give them good opportunity to make their wedding plans, and Angela and Andrea would talk during the week about how they would pull it off jointly. Tiny had no delusions about his role in this wedding plan.

"You know," he said to Danny as they cruised along on the interstate, "Our two fiancées will have this all figured out by the time I pick Angela up at Pittsburgh International on Friday."

Danny nodded vigorously. "Yup, all we have to do is practice saying 'Yes, dear.' And make sure you can say it without hesitation or quavering. They'll want enthusiastic agreement to whatever they've decided."

"Still," Tiny smiled his huge grin, "would you ever, ever, have imagined that we would both meet such remarkable women on the same week's vacation, fall headlong in love, and get ourselves engaged? I mean, what *are* the odds, bro'?"

"Beyond computation, my friend, astronomical to the limitlessness of infinity. I've said it countless times during the years of my ministry, with God nothing is impossible, but this has to be miracle with a capital 'M'."

Tiny again couldn't help breaking out into his deep bass voice, "Love is in the air-r-r."

And even though his singing voice was so bad that the choir directors of his churches had always banned him from the choir room, Danny joined in with his 'joyful' noise... "And get us to the church on tim-m-me." It was easily the most enjoyable cross-country drive the two had ever experienced.

CHAPTER TWENTY-THREE

Monday after an early light supper at home, Danny went to his Pastor's Study at South Presbyterian Church to check on notes and messages that had probably accumulated during his week away in Northern Michigan. One was a message from his therapist, Linda Mulligan, asking if he could move his appointment up to earlier Tuesday afternoon, at 1:30. *Boy, is she gonna be surprised at what I have to report,* Danny thought to himself with delight.

Another message was from Tim Murphy, saying that while Mark and he would be there for their pre-wedding conference with Danny at 7:30 as planned, Tim wanted to talk to Danny prior to then, and would come at 7:00, with Mark joining them later. It was marked, "Urgent." Danny wondered what that was about, but he didn't have to wait long to find out, because a few minutes before 7:00 Tim walked through the side door of the church into the office area. Danny noticed that rather than joyful and enthusiastic, as one would expect Tim to be just days away from his long-delayed marriage to Mark, his face looked troubled and nervous.

The two pastors and friends exchanged "How was your

trip?" and "How did things go while I was away?" with unusually terse answers before Tim got to the point.

"I'm afraid there were 'incidents' while you were gone," Tim shared ominously.

"Okay," Danny responded, "we all know that the mice will play while the cat's away. What was it this time? The deacons get in trouble with the Women's Association again for taking pots and pans out of the church kitchen to use at their cookout?" He made light of the fact that just such a "pots and pans" brouhaha had occurred earlier in the summer when the deacons had applied entirely too much logic to the facts that it was a church kitchen, after all, and that the pots and pans belonged to the church as a whole. So why wouldn't they be able to use them at a church picnic, wash them, and return them to their usual storage places? But they had acted without accounting for the assumed authority of certain women who unflinchingly regarded it as "Their Kitchen." The spat had gone on for weeks, and the Women's Association ladies still hissed about it to anyone who didn't scurry away in time.

But Tim didn't even smile or shake his head at the reference. "No, it was Buck Gibson, Bob Banks, their wives, probably, maybe some others of their PUP's." He cited the usual players who had been agitating from time to time at the church and elsewhere in behalf of Presbyterians United for Purity. "They had heard about the elders approving the use of the church and the sanctuary for our wedding this coming Saturday and they went ballistic."

"What happened?" Danny asked him.

"Well, the first Sunday of your vacation break, when you had just arrived in Northern Michigan, Buck came into the sanctuary just as the service was starting, carrying one of their placards – "Adam and Eve, Not Steve!" He just stood in the back, holding it, glowering silently at me in the pulpit. I did what we talked about and just ignored him, so long as he wasn't being loud and disruptive of the service. As people were leaving at the conclusion of worship, he posted himself at the bottom of the front steps. I was greeting people at the door, shaking hands, thanking them for coming. But when they went down the steps, he confronted them at the bottom, denouncing the 'abomination' of same-sex marriage. He was particularly agitated when he spotted church officers coming out of worship and would argue with them about their decision to approve use of the church for Mark's and my wedding next Saturday."

"Were there others with him?"

"His wife, Brenda, was there, but she didn't do anything but whisper among some of her friends, shaking heads. I didn't see Bob Banks or his wife, Mary. I didn't bother you on your vacation because it was relatively limited in scope. Some people were obviously bothered by the incident. Some seemed to take what Buck was saying seriously, but most just brushed by him, not giving him the time of day. I could see he was frustrated that not more would listen to him."

Danny sensed there was more to share. "Go on, what else happened?"

"The next thing was on Wednesday, during the kids' midweek program early that evening. I was in the Fellowship Hall, coordinating the recreation for the grade school youngsters, and one of our adult volunteers saw Brenda Gibson out in the parking lot, going around my car. When there was a break in the kids' activities, I went out there, thinking that maybe she had stuck a nasty note under my windshield wiper or something, but found all four of my tires flat. Now no one reported actually seeing her deflating them, but the assumption is that it was her doing. And she may also have been the one who 'keyed' the word 'Homo' on my car door."

"Did you report that to the police?"

"Yes, again following the policies we had set up, I phoned them. A patrol car came out; the two officers looked at the flat tires and scratches, and they filled out an incident report. Since no one had seen Brenda doing the deed, nor anyone else, of course, they said that they could contact the Gibson's and question them about it, but probably wouldn't have enough to make an arrest. Again, it was annoying and resulted in some expense for me, but not that big of a deal. I told your friend, Detective Sergeant Bradley, that I would be sure to report any further incidents, especially if there seemed to be an accelerating pattern."

"And was there? Any additional trouble from the PUP's?"

"After the Wednesday evening incident, each day following, Thursday through Saturday, there were phone calls with messages left, both at the church and at our home. The calls were always when we wouldn't be there to answer the phone, at the church office after everyone had left for the day, at home when both Mark and I were at work. The voice would always be somewhat distorted, and not the same voice each time, but the messages were fairly consistent. If we knew what was good for us, we'd cancel the wedding, or the wrath of God will come down on us for our sins...stuff like that."

"And did you report the phone calls, too?"

"I know, I should have," Tim confessed, "but I'm afraid I got angry by the second and third day, and just deleted them as fast as I could. I particularly hated to have Mildred hear that stuff when she would come to work in the office, or for Mark to have to listen to it. He already wonders if he should just call the courthouse and arrange for us to exchange our vows there. He hates to have the church impacted so negatively."

"Well, we're not going to give in to those cowards," Danny

stated firmly. "Nobody is doing anything wrong. From our local board of elders to the national level of the Presbyterian Church, USA, your wedding plans are approved and are according to state law. I'll call Jim Bradley Tuesday morning and let him know that this seems to be an ongoing pattern of harassment and illegal activity. Maybe he would see to it that more frequent patrols are made Friday evening during your rehearsal and Saturday for the marriage service, even post some unobtrusive police presence to keep a low-key eye on things. I'll see what he thinks. Now Mark will be here any minute, so let's have a good planning session with him. And he needs to be filled in on what's been going on, you know."

"You're right," Tim agreed. "He knows some of it, but it's wrong for me to think I can somehow shelter him from all of this."

"And how did yesterday's worship go? Any more incidents?"

"Surprisingly, no. The elders, the church staff, and I all braced ourselves in anticipation that maybe Buck and Bob would gather a bunch of their supporters and stage a rowdy picketing or demonstration. A patrol car parked down the street a bit, I think to assure that people could get into the church and out again without assault, but none of the troublemakers showed up. There was one thing, though," Tim admitted. "The last threatening phone call on Saturday night left a message that said simply, 'You've had your last warning. We're not responsible for what comes upon you.' I refused to be intimidated, however, and just deleted it."

But Danny did not think lightly about the matter. *What is it they intend to come upon us?*

CHAPTER TWENTY-FOUR

The pre-wedding conference with Tim and Mark was much lighter in mood. After he reported to Danny what had gone on in his absence, Tim relaxed more. Mark and he were obviously a couple very much in love. Various subjects were discussed under Danny's leadership: the sacredness of their union about to occur, God's love for them individually and as spouses, the new family they were beginning together, including whether they had any intentions of pursuing adoption of one or more children and subsequent parent roles that would result. All three of them became more joyful and enthusiastic about the wedding they were planning. Mark seemed reassured about having the ceremony at the church, encouraged by Danny. Tim felt less edgy about the PUP problems, feeling certain that Danny and the police would keep things under control. And Danny felt simply thankful to be a part of such love and union before God.

There were no harassing phone calls at the church that night, but Danny had no illusions that the problem had just gone away. The PUP's were typical of people in church and society who become zealous to an extreme about whatever "cause" they embrace. An evil fanaticism can take hold, and they seem to descend into a kind of "tunnel vision" where their cause overshadows all other concerns. They lose the ability to see anything else around them, including common sense, respect and consideration for others, their obligations as citizens in a society based on laws, and most of all, the reality of a God who loves and cares completely for each and every person on the planet, or in the universe. Danny knew that vigilance and caution would be necessary for the days ahead.

CHAPTER TWENTY-FIVE

Tuesday afternoon at 1:27 p.m. Danny arrived at the office of his therapist, Linda Mulligan. They sat in comfortable chairs across from each other at a round coffee table.

"Tell me about your trip to Northern Michigan," Linda began. "How do you think it went for you?"

Danny proceeded to tell her about the visit Tiny and he made to the old Brand summer home, and how he thought viewing the scene of his captivity and the attempt on his life actually helped. It was significantly different now, and seeing it again aided in accepting that it was no longer a place of danger for him.

Linda smiled and nodded, encouraging him to continue to express his feelings. Danny went on, then, to relate the shooting incident at the end of the sporting clays course that Sunday, as well as his meeting Andrea for the first time.

"Right after that shot passed by me so closely at the Cedar Club, I have to confess that I wondered if it would awaken those bad memories, the strong feelings of anxiety and danger, but it really didn't. For one thing, I had no reason to feel as though I was the target. If anyone was, it would probably have been Andrea, who was standing close to me, facing me. But for another thing, even though I had just met her, I think deep feelings were already stirring within me. Could my beginning feelings for Andrea have been so strong as to ward off the possible intrusion of my old anxiety?"

"That's not only very possible," Linda agreed, "but just what we would hope for, that good, beautiful, positive energy would bolster your thoughts and feelings to provide impenetrable defenses against the resurgence of your traumatized memories. So long as you believe your feelings for this woman to be authentic, I would definitely embrace them. If you decide it's really love, well, there's no better healing power, no better protective shield in the dangers of life, than love."

Danny had to go on, of course, to relate that he had very quickly decided that what he was feeling was true love such as he had not experienced since his late wife Samantha had passed on.

"In fact," he almost confessed, "each minute of each hour of each day I was there in Northern Michigan I felt myself falling deeper and deeper in love with Andrea. I kid you not, it was like the two of us were interlocking pieces of life's puzzle, just waiting to be put together to complete the wondrous picture. By the time Tiny and I were about to leave Traverse City and drive back here, I asked her to marry me, and she accepted. Do you think I acted too hastily?"

"Well, Daniel," Linda leaned back a bit in her chair and spoke thoughtfully and carefully, "that's a question only you can answer. Was it a quick romance? Certainly, people would probably say so, but there is no defined timetable, no exact formula, when it comes to love. A couple of days have passed since the two of you became engaged. How do you feel about it now?"

"I've never been more certain of anything in my entire life. I've lived over half a century at this point, and in all those years I have never felt more right in a decision, and certainly no happier. I believe this is God's will for me, and that God has provided us for each other."

"Well then," she concluded, "I think you've answered your own question. If the two of you share such a love and commitment to be partners in all that life might bring to you, then I'm very happy for you. I wish the best of everything for the two of you," she smiled and congratulated him.

CHAPTER TWENTY-SIX

Danny had a lot to catch up on during the rest of the week. There were meetings at the church, hospital visits, phone calls to return, a sermon to write for the next Sunday's worship, lots of other tasks, but by late Friday afternoon he felt reasonably caught up with most things in his work and ministry. Tiny had talked with him on the phone during the week but was also catching up on work and developments on the Hill during his absence. Angela was flying in late Friday afternoon, and Tiny and Slick had gone to the airport to get her. Slick drove Tiny's big, black Lincoln, and even had fun with it by donning a black chauffeur's cap. Tiny and Angela sat in the back seats and enjoyed their reunion while Slick took them to the Hilton in downtown Pittsburgh, where Tiny had reserved a suite for the two of them, as he said he would.

They checked in just in time to have their bags put up in the suite and have Slick join them for a quick, light supper in the hotel restaurant. Then they drove to South Presbyterian Church for the 7:30 rehearsal. Tim had insisted that they be included as honored guests at the rehearsal and for desserts and wine afterward at the nearby Embassy Suites. Tim had gotten acquainted with Danny's long-time friend and protector, Tiny, but had someone asked him about it, he was *really* looking forward to meeting this Angela, whom Danny had described to him as one of the most beautiful women on earth...next to Andrea, of course.

The rehearsal went smoothly, was both serious and fun, as rehearsals should be, and once again there were no incidents from the direction of the PUP's. Danny was on the one hand grateful, but on the other hand found the "quiet" to be somehow ominous. He hoped and prayed that Saturday would also be quiet, incident-free, and feature nothing but love and joy. The rehearsal reception did not go late, and since Andrea had worked that day but was off for Friday evening, Danny, Tiny, and Angela called her, put her on speaker, and let her know that while they were having fun, they wished she was there with them.

"Aw, I wish I was there, too, guys," Andrea assured them. "You have to promise me that the next wedding any of us attends will be for the four of us," she laughed.

"Angela's not flying back to Michigan until Monday morning," Tiny said, "So while we'll be busy tomorrow with Tim and Mark's wedding and reception, and that will probably go into the night, we thought the three of us could call you back Sunday afternoon."

"Yeah," Danny jumped in, "I'll be leading our two services at South Presbyterian that morning, and you'll be singing in the choir at your Traverse City church, but after lunch on Sunday, say about 2:00, we can call you back. That sound okay?"

"Sounds great," Andrea agreed. "And Angela...."

"I'm here, girl, go ahead," Angela replied.

"Be sure to take mental notes and pictures at the wedding tomorrow, ideas for our own wedding. We have to act quickly if we're going to pull it off as soon as the first week in October. And good luck with our two guys there. They're quite a handful, but if anyone can keep them under control, you can, Angela."

"Not to worry," Danny intervened. "All Angela has to do is give a little whistle and Tiny comes running, ready to obey, like a giant lap dog. And he keeps me in line."

Tiny gave him a playful whack but smiled compliantly at Angela. There was truth in what Danny said. He had never wanted to please anyone so much in his life as this dear woman.

CHAPTER TWENTY-SEVEN

The marriage service early Saturday afternoon was reverent, moving, and had grace and beauty. It centered on God's blessing of Mark and Tim's union, was well-attended by their family members, and included a considerable number of church members. Everyone and anyone in the congregation had been invited. And Tiny and Angela sat in a front pew, right behind Tim's family. The truly happy couple joined arms after Danny's benediction and recessed down the center isle to the rousing strains of "Joyful, Joyful, We Adore Thee."

Tiny and Angela were escorted down the aisle by ushers immediately after Tim's family and relatives and were encouraged to join the receiving line down the church steps and the front walk. Wedding party members and Mark's family joined in to make a long line to greet guests with smiles and hugs. Lots of photos were snapped, and multi-colored confetti was tossed as the newly-weds came down the line to receive their congratulations and best wishes from all.

Danny surveyed the joyous scene from the big, outer doors of the church. Looking out over the assemblage, all he could see was happy celebration. There were no protestors, no signs and demonstrations to taint the festive mood, no Buck or Bob or any of their group that he could see as he scanned around. Maybe they had retreated from their cowardly threats and stunts when they realized that the wedding was not going to be called off. Danny was relieved that he didn't have to deal with their bigotry and bombast, but he still had an uneasy feeling that they were being *too* quiet.

Garbed in his black pulpit robe with its three velvet stripes on each sleeve and a white, gold-embroidered, fringed stole around his neck and down the front of the robe, Danny went down to join Mark, Tim, Tiny and Angela as they clustered for a moment on the walk, hugging and rejoicing.

The Angel of Death sped up the front walk of the church easily as fast as the approaching bullet. The .308, 168-grain, boat-tailed bullet ripped through voluminous sleeve of Danny's robe from the back as he put his arm around Angela, struck her in the upper torso, and tore through soft flesh to hit Mark standing in front of them as they were giving congratulations.

The Angel invisibly gathered the exiting soul in what would have seemed like a great vessel scooping up a lone drop as it fell from the body, if it were possible to give bodily form to the purely spiritual event. The Angel and the soul swept instantly into the timelessness of Eternity, into the spiritual Kingdom of Heaven, before the dead shell of the victim had even struck the walk and lawn below it.

CHAPTER TWENTY-EIGHT

As the bullet struck, the sharp *crack* of the rifle was heard across the street and up the hillside from the front of the church. Mere reflex caused Danny to look up that way, where at the top of the hill there was a Seven-Eleven and gas station. At the same time, he was grabbing for Angela as she began to topple, but he thought he saw a split-second glimpse of Buck Gibson scrambling into his pickup truck by the parking lot fence a couple of hundred yards or more away. But his attention returned quickly to Angela's bleeding body as she slumped down to the grass next to the walk. Tiny immediately put his big arm underneath her head and cradled her as he moaned.

"No, no, Angela. Angela, can you hear me? Hang on, baby. You'll be okay."

Wedding guests milled around in fear and confusion, some running for their cars, some gathering around the victims, some practically frozen in place, their heads spinning around trying to figure out what was happening. Down the block the Pittsburgh police officers had heard the shot, saw the chaotic crowd in front of the church, threw to-go cups of coffee on the ground, and drove up to the church quickly with lights flashing and a blast of siren. Danny motioned for those nearest to back up and give room for the officers, who had already called for backup and emergency vehicles.

Then he noticed Mark on the pavement as well, with Tim hunched over him, wailing and hugging the inert form of his new spouse. A physician among the wedding guests came forward rapidly to check the victims, and everyone gave her room to work. The police officers moved people further back, while scanning the hill above with their weapons drawn, ready to respond if there was any more shooting. The pickup truck had already left the Seven-Eleven parking lot above them, and no other possible threat could be seen.

Danny, Tiny, and a nurse present helped with clean cloths that someone had thoughtfully run into the church to get, dashing back to the scene as quickly as possible. The physician put pressure on Angela's chest wound, had Tiny hold the cloth in place, while she and the nurse turned to Mark. Mark showed no pulse, so CPR was initiated immediately while pressure was also placed on his wounds.

"I still can't feel a pulse," the nurse announced as the doctor made compressions. Off in the distance the sirens of the approaching ambulances and fire truck could be heard coming closer. Soon emergency medical technicians had portable gurneys and stabilizing supports unloaded and rushed to the victims. Both Mark and Angela were attended to and loaded into the ambulances to be hurried to Shadyside Hospital on Centre Ave., not far off Baum Boulevard, and the closest to South Presbyterian Church.

Meanwhile, more police cars, officers, and detectives were arriving to secure the scene and the surrounding area. Danny felt better seeing Detective Sergeant Jim Bradley arriving to take charge of the investigation.

"Jim, thank God you're here. I have to get out of this robe

and get to the hospital."

"You go ahead," the sergeant sent him off. "There'll be detectives there to take your statements. We're going to canvass, look for clues, all the evidence we can find. And Dr. Henriks, don't you worry; we'll get to the bottom of this."

CHAPTER TWENTY-NINE

On his drive to the hospital Danny had of course called Andrea on his Bluetooth to let her know of the tragedy at the wedding. She was horrified and distraught.

"I'm still off until Monday. Shall I get a ticket and fly out of Cherry Capital ASAP? I can get a hold of my lieutenant and request some days off starting next Monday."

"That'd be great, hon," Danny replied. "But why don't you wait a bit until I have more to tell you. I'll keep you informed. We'll figure out together what might be best to do. I'll know more when I can get to the hospital."

When Danny reached the hospital, he went straight to the emergency room. He identified himself to the head nurse as the Presbyterian pastor at whose church the shooting had just occurred.

"What can you tell me about the victims? The woman's name is Angela, can I see her?"

"Her wound was well-treated by the physician on the scene and the EMT's, but she was taken into surgery as soon as she got here to repair a tear in a branch of the left pulmonary artery. She was stable going in, and one of our best thoracic and vascular surgeons was available to do the repair. Does she have any family members here?"

"No, she has no family here, but her fiancé should be here somewhere – tall, big, African-American fellow, thoroughly distraught."

"Oh, he must be the one I saw in the surgery waiting room. You should find him there."

"Well, first," Danny stopped her, "what about the second victim – the man?"

"I'm sorry to say, pastor, but he was pronounced DOA. At the scene and in the ambulance. They were never able to get a pulse after he was shot. He probably was dead before he hit the ground. Does he have any family here?"

"Yes, his spouse should also be here, or on the way, as well as his parents and other family members. I'll look for them, too."

Danny quickly found Tiny, tears running down his cheeks, wringing his hands. Tiny looked up as his best friend approached.

"This can't be happening. God wouldn't take her from me so soon after giving her to me. Is she gonna be okay, Danny? Tell me she'll be okay."

"She's in surgery," Danny replied, mustering up as much confidence and control as he could under the circumstances. "The head nurse said that her surgeon is one of their best, that he's repairing a tear in an artery. She was stable and doing well when she went in, and I think we can hope for the best. The surgeon will come out to speak to us as soon as he's able."

Tiny just nodded his head to indicate that he had heard all that, but hunched over and weepy, it seemed to Danny that he had never seen the big man look so small and vulnerable. Danny put his arm around Tiny's shoulders and sat with him until he saw Tim and Mark's parents out in the hall. A doctor was talking to them, and although Danny couldn't hear what the physician was saying, Tim buried his head in his hands and sobbed violently. Mark's mom turned and collapsed into the arms of her weeping husband.

Danny asked Tiny if he'd be okay for a moment while he stepped out, got an affirmative nod, and went to Tim and Mark's parents.

"Words can't express how terribly sorry I am," Danny said to them, his voice wavering as he experienced his own tears. There were no words that could suffice, nor change what had happened. There was just hugging, crying, and holding on to the love that would endure even across the chasm of Death. Not since his late wife Samantha had died had Danny leaned so entirely on the promise of St. Paul that "neither death nor life, nor angels nor rulers, nor things present nor things to come...will ever be able to separate us from the love of God in Christ Jesus our Lord." Nor from the love of each other. They kept clinging to each other and to that divine love. Danny prayed softly for all of them, and especially for the departed soul of Mark.

Promising that he would get in touch with all of them soon, Danny returned to sit with Tiny in the waiting room. It seemed like the proverbial eternity on earth before the surgeon came out, his mask crumpled at his throat.

"She did fine. The surgery went well, and we believe the arterial tear is repaired. She's in recovery but will be transferred to ICU soon. She lost quite a bit of blood, but transfusions have helped with that. We'll see that she gets the best, 24-hour care, and transfer her to a regular room as soon as we feel certain she's ready."

"I want a private room for her, and a private nurse with her always," Tiny spoke up.

"You can put in that request. I'm sure a private room can be available. A private nurse would be redundant, however," the surgeon assured him. "She'll be monitored constantly, and immediate care will always be available to her. Feel free to ask for me if I can answer any questions or if you have any concerns."

The surgeon left, and Danny reassured Tiny. "It sounds good. I'm sure she's going to be okay. I'll stay with you and we can see her as soon as she's awake."

"Thanks, man," Tiny was truly grateful, "but you should get back to the church. You have services to lead tomorrow. Besides, the best thing you can do for us right now is pray for Angela. And check with your detective sergeant on what they've found. I want this bastard found, and if they don't arrest him soon, my old crew and I will hunt him down and take care of it ourselves."

Danny understood full well the indescribable feelings behind that rising voice and rage. He thought that today's Tiny would rely upon the police and the entire justice system to handle the matter. But he also knew that deep, down inside there had to be remnants of the old Tiny who would have employed "street justice" if he had the chance.

"Okay, brother," Danny agreed. "I'll leave for now. You be sure to call me on my cell with any update or change. I'll get things squared away at the church, check in with Jim Bradley, find out what's going on, and be back here for you two early this evening. Sound good?"

Tiny nodded vigorously, waved thankfully, and resumed his slumped-over misery and prayers. Danny had just never seen him like that before. Nothing in the world ever intimidated Tiny...except now his fear for Angela...and any possibility that he could lose her.

CHAPTER THIRTY

Danny called Andrea back to update her on Angela and, regrettably, to tell her the bad news about Mark.

"Oh, that's so sad. I never had a chance to meet him, or Tim, but I feel so sorry for them. But I'm thankful for the encouraging prognosis for Angela. I've been praying nonstop for her and Tiny."

Danny could hear the tearfulness in her voice, but then the very professional shift to her law enforcement demeanor.

"You probably haven't heard anything about the police investigation yet but be sure and let me know whatever they tell you. Are they good there?"

"Thankfully, yes," Danny replied. "Detective Sergeant Jim Bradley is in charge, and there probably isn't any better investigator. I've been a volunteer police chaplain for the department for years. And have known him all that time."

"Well, I wish I was there for all of you. I could still fly out there."

"And I wish you were here, too, Andrea, but let's hold off until we know a bit more and figure out what's best to do. Okay?"

"Okay," she agreed. "But I'll let them know here that I

may need some emergency time off, just in case. Call me back soon."

"I will. And I love you more than anything."

"Me, too...love you."

Danny got to the church. The police were still there, conducting their investigation. The detective hadn't caught up to him at the hospital to get his statement, so right away Sergeant Bradley interviewed him. He got Danny's version of what had happened, including his glimpse of the man he was sure was Buck Gibson, getting in his truck up in the Seven-Eleven parking lot above them and hurriedly driving away.

"I can tell you," Jim Bradley shared with Danny, "that the CSI team found a .308 shell up there by the dumpster, and they've located the lead slug that passed through both the woman and the man. As soon as we can find the rifle, we can produce a forensic match. They've also taken casts of footprints near the fence, and photos of tread marks on the asphalt from that truck you saw speeding away. I'll put a BOLO out for that Gibson fellow. We'll find him and find out who did this if it wasn't him."

Danny thanked him, and the sergeant turned away to receive information from an officer who had just come up to him. Danny felt shaken returning to the still-bloody scene but put on his own professional demeanor and went in the side door of the church to the office area, then into his study. His long-time custodian, Mel, had left a note saying that he would see to it that all was cleaned up and ready for Sunday services. Then he noticed the red light was on at his desk phone. He picked up the receiver and punched in the code to pick up the message. The soft, gravelly West Virginia accent was Buck Gibson's.

"Pastor, we have to talk. No police. Just meet me out at the gun club, ASAP...please."

CHAPTER THIRTY-ONE

Danny hung up the receiver and thought hard. He knew he should go back out and tell Jim Bradley about this message. He considered calling Andrea and asking her what he should do. He couldn't call Tiny. He had all he could handle waiting and praying for Angela to make it out of surgery and recovery. Besides, if the big guy learned of this message, he would descend upon the Keystone Rod & Gun Club with a fury like that of the Avenging Angel unleashed. If he did as Buck asked, he could be walking into a trap. After all, he was the one common denominator for the shootings both in Northern Michigan and here in Pittsburgh. He had the strong feeling that *he* was the intended target...and that the would-be killer was determined enough to hunt him down anywhere in the country.

On the other hand, Danny thought, Buck's voice in the message did not come across as threatening or particularly ominous. On the contrary, he sounded scared and pleading. Could it be that someone was trying to set Buck up to take the fall for the shooting? But who? Another of the PUP's trying to oust Buck? Or the same man who used Wes Smith as a patsy at the Cedar Club and now is using Buck? Or was

Buck the one who put Wes up to that stunt, and is he now trying to lure the pastor he holds in contempt by pretending to sound desperate? Buck's West Virginia accent was rather Southern in tone. All the possibilities made Danny feel dizzy and confused.

There was no way he could figure out the answer by himself. No, he should pass it on to Jim Bradley and let the experts do the investigating. On the other hand, Buck had to have set up careful surveillance out at the Keystone Club. He specified "no police," so whether by himself or with the help of others, he would be watching all approaches to the shooting range for arriving vehicles other than Danny's Grand Cherokee. A shooter and hunter himself, Buck had long-range optics. If he spotted or even suspected a police presence, Buck would surely take an immediate exit route.

In fact, why would Buck even chance a meeting with me when he knew that he had to be suspect number one? Why would he put himself at risk for apprehension by the police unless he had vital information, something important to share? His tone really struck me as sincere and pleading. Maybe I should first find out what Buck wanted. If I actually succeed in meeting and talking with Buck, and found out more, well, he certainly couldn't get very far by the time I would make the call to the police.

Danny admitted to himself that he probably wasn't exercising the best judgment, but he finally decided that he would chance the meeting with Buck. He would take his own precautions, however: be extremely careful in his approach to the club, have Jim Bradley keyed up for immediate call on his cell phone...and one more thing.

First Danny left the church quietly, drove quickly to his South Hills home, and got his Ruger .22 handgun out of his gun safe. It was strictly a short-range weapon that he used only for pistol range target shooting, but he shot expertly with it, and in a close encounter he knew that he could put a bullet right between the eyes of any assailant. He had maintained a Concealed Weapons Permit for years, despite almost never carrying a concealed handgun, so he put a middle-of-the-back belt holster on under his jacket and slipped the Ruger into it. Danny had never shot at a human being in his life, and certainly didn't want to now, but he would be ready for whatever Buck had in mind.

CHAPTER THIRTY-TWO

Danny slowed down as soon as the Keystone Rod & Gun Club came into view in the distance. He stopped his Jeep and got out with his ten-power Leupold binoculars. He scanned the club buildings and grounds, the parking lot and the roadsides near the club fencing. Soon he spotted Buck Gibson's pickup truck, parked on the far side of the parking lot, near the fence. No other vehicles were around, since the club was closed by early Saturday evening.

Danny stayed put and continued to watch through the field glasses. Finally, he spotted a figure crouched on the far side of the parked truck, but it didn't look like Buck. No, he finally determined that it was his wife, Brenda. She seemed to be sitting on a little folding stool, just looking and waiting. Danny watched some more, scanning a couple of more times, failed to see anyone else, and then decided that he would get back into the Jeep and drive cautiously up to the Gibson's truck.

As soon as she saw the Grand Cherokee approaching, Brenda Gibson got up and waved at Danny. He pulled up several yards away, continuing to be on high alert and swiveling his head around, looking for Buck or any possible threat. He still couldn't see anyone else.

As he carefully got out of his vehicle, Danny kept close watch on Brenda, but kept glancing around suspiciously.

"Pastor, oh, thank you for coming," Brenda said. "I'm so scared...we both are..."

"Mrs. Gibson," Danny interrupted her, "what's going on here? Where's Buck? He left a message for me saying that he and I had to talk, that he wanted to meet me here. So, where is he?"

"He's nearby," she assured him. "Did you bring the police or anyone else? We're so scared," she repeated. "Has anyone followed you?"

Danny didn't want to give away too much, and certainly not that he was foolish enough to come to this peculiar meeting alone, so he decided not to answer her questions.

"If you can," Danny instructed, "just let Buck know I'm here, and that he should come out of hiding, or else I'm leaving immediately."

"Oh, he knows you're here. He's keeping close watch, just like God's watching over us all the time, like he always does for his chosen ones. But we're weak, and so we're scared, but I'll signal Buck to come down."

She stepped out to the edge of the road and waved vigorously in the opposite direction from which Danny had come just then. After a few minutes of standing and watching in that direction – though Danny kept scanning as best he could in all directions – another figure started to emerge from the dense thickets off the road on the far side. The man was dressed completely in camouflage, from his boot tops to a face veil and floppy hat, but Danny was sure it was Buck.

As Buck Gibson drew closer to the two of them, Danny focused hard to try to see if he was carrying any sort of weapon, while slipping his own hand within easy reach of his back holster. As Buck came up to them, he slipped off both his hat and his face veil so that Danny could see that it was he. Danny also saw a face that was sweating profusely and seemed contorted with pain and anxiety.

"Pastor, thank you so much for coming," Buck said. "I really didn't think you would. I'm sorry for dragging you out here to Hannastown like this, but we really have to talk."

"I have a lot of questions for you, Buck," Danny said sharply, "beginning with whether you were the one who fired that shot early this afternoon at the church? If it was you, you should know that an innocent person is dead because of it."

"Oh no, no, that wasn't me. Sure, I admit that I was in the parking lot up by the Seven-Eleven, but I didn't take that shot. I didn't even have a gun with me."

"If that's true," Danny continued, "why were you there? What were you up to? And if you're not the shooter, do you know who was?"

"Look, Pastor, you know that Brenda, our friends and I have been strongly opposed to the abomination of having homosexuals in our church. And the elders and you okaying that homo wedding for today is a sin against God and God's inerrant Law – the Bible says so – but the Bible also says not to take judgment into our own hands: 'Thou shalt not kill.' So, yes, I was up there, but I was just there to keep watch. I didn't want to be down close, lest anyone think that I was in any way a part of that sinning, so I just looked from on high."

Danny overlooked Buck's bigoted interpretation of biblical materials and his language. This was not the time to discuss or debate such matters of distorted belief, but he pressed Buck harder on just what happened, and who was responsible for the fatal shooting.

"I'll repeat myself. If it wasn't you, was it one of your group? What happened up there?"

"There were, oh, probably three or four other cars up there with me in that lot. One was parked way down on the far end, close to the fence overlooking the hillside and the church down below. I didn't pay much attention to the other vehicles, because, to be honest, I was taking photos and making notes on the whole travesty going on at the church, all those nonbelievers coming out of the so-called 'wedding,' the reveling like it was Sodom and Gomorrah of old. I could see all of you gathered along the front walk, when I heard that shot. I knew right away that it was a hunting rifle, and I saw people fall down next to you in your robe.

"Well, of course I glanced down the way and saw a man holding a rifle, scrambling away from the fence. He threw it in the back of his car, then jumped into the driver's side and wheeled around and down the street. Nobody else was in the lot at the time, and I don't think anyone else saw him, but I swear to God Almighty that was what happened."

"But you didn't stick around to tell the police or anyone," Danny said accusingly, "so how do I know you just didn't make this up and that you weren't really the shooter?"

"Hey," Brenda jumped in defensively, "would my hubby and I bother calling you and meeting like this unless it was true? My man doesn't lie," she scowled at Danny's accusation.

Actually, Danny thought, *she has a point*. What would be the sense of risking a meeting and conversation like this if it was all contrived? Forensic evidence should soon verify as to whether the shot came from a Gibson gun or not, and whether the trajectory of the shot came from where Buck was standing by the fence. But why bother with calling him out for this strained meeting?

"Okay," Danny gave grudgingly, "let's suppose it was as you say. Why not just go right to the police, tell it all to them, let them check for evidence that would clear you and your guns of any wrongdoing? Why was it so important to talk one-on-one with me first?"

"Pastor," Ward sounded less defensive and almost apologetic, "you and I have been at odds on this homo stuff. Again, I admit that I believe you have been a false teacher. Like the Bible says, frankly, a wolf who comes among the sheep and leads them astray. But I have never wanted any real harm to come to you or anyone else about all this. Okay, there have been a few scuffles when we Presbyterians United for Purity have tried to get folks' attention and open their eyes to the Revealed Truth, but nobody's ever gotten seriously hurt, and certainly not anyone killed. Am I not right?"

Danny wasn't inclined to give him any "wiggle room" or any positive points concerning his bigotry. "Go on," he pushed Buck.

"Well, I figured that whether anyone spotted me up there by the Seven-Eleven at the time of the shot or not, I would certainly be a prime suspect, and a lot of time would be spent harassing me, my woman, and my friends among the PUP's, time that would be better spent looking for the real perp, so I wanted to get my story out ASAP. And I wanted you to know that while I may oppose you and your heresy, as a man of God myself, I would not do something like this. My word is true, so help me God."

For all of Buck Gibson's presumed self-righteousness, there was also a continuing plea and a tone of desperation in what he said and how he said it. He obviously wanted Danny to accept what he was saying, and especially that he was innocent of the crime and the death. Nonetheless, while Danny himself was not Buck and Brenda's Final Judge for their sin, he simply could not let them off the hook for their hatred, their bigotry, their meanness, their troublemaking, their judgmental spirit. And probably most of all, their inability to love others, no matter who they are, or how different they may seem.

"Okay," Danny continued, "If you saw this other man, holding a rifle, what did he look like?"

"It happened so fast I didn't get a really good look, but I figure he was about average height, maybe in his 50's, about your age. He had a cap on, but I could see gray hair sticking out. Mm-m, that's about all...oh, sunglasses or shooting glasses, you know, yellow-tinted. Blue windbreaker, khaki pants."

Danny shook his head, took a few steps back to his Jeep, and then turned back to the couple. "If you had really wanted the authorities not to have to waste time and effort tracking you down instead of the real shooter, you would have gone to them with what you know immediately. What I think of you or know about you in all of this is not the point. What matters is what the police need to know, and what God knows of your heart, your thoughts, your words, and your actions."

"I'm going to them, next," Buck insisted. "They can examine my guns, put me on a polygraph, do whatever they must to confirm my innocence."

"Yeah," Brenda chimed in, "we're the good guys here."

Danny couldn't help himself. Even pastors yield to temptation. As he started to drive away, he leaned out of his open window and looked out at the two.

"If I were you, I'd just stay parked right where you are. The police will be here any minute. I called them as soon as I pulled up and saw your truck here," he stretched the truth. "They'll decide whether you're good guys or not, but you sure as hell aren't in my book."

Buck and Brenda shook their heads in disgust and indignation. They were still standing there, looking both angry and forlorn, as he looked back in his rearview mirror. But he agreed. Buck was most likely innocent of the shooting.

CHAPTER THIRTY-THREE

Danny called Tiny soon after he left the Keystone Club and the Gibson's and found out that Angela had been transferred out of surgical recovery and into her room at ICU. He promised that he would be back to the hospital soon. He then called Jim Bradley on his cell phone to let him know of the whereabouts of Buck Gibson.

"And you know this how, chaplain?" the sergeant demanded.

Danny proceeded to tell him of the meeting at the gun club with the Gibson's. "I know I shouldn't have gone, but...."

"You're damn right you shouldn't have," the normally cool and collected detective exploded. "I swear to God, Dr. Henriks, I'm going to put you into protective custody for your own good at this rate. Don't you ever again.... you know what, when you get back here I have in mind to have you arrested for obstructing in a police investigation. Damn it, you think I want another body on my hands?"

Danny felt like his cell phone was sizzling against his ear with the barrage from his detective sergeant friend. He winced while Bradley turned to an officer standing nearby to put out more information on his previously-issued BOLO for Buck Gibson.

"Seal off all routes from the Keystone Rod & Gun Club," Bradley ordered. "Road blocks and all available cars. Consider the suspect to be armed and dangerous." He turned back to his conversation with Danny. "And as for you, *former* Police Chaplain...."

"Jim, Jim...you're breaking up. Must be the mountains...I'll be back to the hospital soon...later." Danny clicked off the cell phone and tossed it on the center console like it was the proverbial hot potato. He was sure his friend Jim would cool off before long, but in the meantime maybe he'd better give him a wide berth.

But he picked up the phone again and knew he had to make an even tougher call – to Andrea. She needed to know how stupid he had been. As soon as she answered her cell, he filled her in on what had happened with the Gibson's. He winced at her response.

"You what? I've fallen in love with a crazy man?" She made it sound more like a statement of fact than a question. "I've waited all these years, thought God would never give me the love of my life, and you...what were you thinking? Clearly you weren't. God forgive me, Daniel Henriks, but if anything had happened to you, I would have dug you up myself, ground your bones into a fine powder, and made cement blocks out of you...which is what your head must be, pulling a stunt like that."

Danny would have considered trying the "you're breaking up" move again, but the fact of the matter was he was paralyzed momentarily by Andrea's righteous anger. She was right. Jim Bradley was right. He had no defense. Although a part of him was glad he had the confrontation with Buck Gibson. He came away from it convinced that however reprehensible the Gibson's and their PUP's were in fact, Buck had not fired the shot that killed Mark and put Angela in the hospital. Clearly Andrea had paused, waiting for him to make some feeble response.

"I know, you're right. I shouldn't have...the last thing I would ever want is for what you and I have to be jeopardiz..."

But she cut him off. "Okay, that settles it. I'm flying out there first flight I can get. I want to be there for Angela and Tiny, and obviously somebody needs to put you in a toddler's harness. I'll call you back as soon as I have flight arrangements. Give me an update as soon as you can on Angela. You know what, I'm going to call Tiny and tell him to sit on you. Then let's see if you can get yourself into more trouble."

Danny was understandably without an available response, except to say, "I love you. Safe travel, hon."

Andrea couldn't help but soften just a smidge, "Love you, too." But she justifiably hardened again, "But I mean it, Daniel, don't you ever again..."

"I won't. Promise. See you soon."

They clicked off with more "love you's." Danny tried to take a breath, feeling like it had all been knocked out of him. He loved Andrea's strength, but made a big mental note that he wanted to try to avoid being the recipient of her righteous anger again. She was one tough cookie. But he had deserved it, and he knew that she truly, irreversibly, loved him. And when he could, he would soon be excited that she was coming, but for now he felt like hiding. He behaved himself in every respect driving back to the hospital, including scrupulously observing all the speed limits, stop signs, and traffic lights.

CHAPTER THIRTY-FOUR

It was early Saturday evening, about 7:00, by the time Danny got back to Shadyside Hospital. He quickly grabbed a sandwich and coffee from the hospital cafeteria and headed up to ICU, where he readily found Tiny sitting with Angela. She was awake now and sitting up, though hooked up to various IV's and monitors.

Tiny turned his head toward Danny as he entered the room, carrying his to-go bag and cup. With an ominously gruff voice, Tiny said, "Andrea called." And while he didn't show it, he smiled inwardly at Danny freezing as if he was that big buck caught in the headlights that evening in Leelanau County.

Danny's eyes widened as he tried to brace for yet another barrage of "what were you thinking?" but Tiny broke into a big grin, got up, and hugged him.

"Angela, look, the prodigal son has returned," Tiny kidded.

Angela smiled weakly and held up her arms with all the lines for a hug, which Danny enthusiastically gave her.

"Ang...I'm so, so glad to see you like this, able to sit up, and even show that beautiful smile again. We've been praying and supporting you with all our love."

Angela nodded thankfully and cheerfully, while Tiny filled Danny in on the latest from the surgeon.

"The surgeon came in again and gave me a fuller report. Thank God and the protective angels that the hard-jacketed bullet passed cleanly through, didn't hit any bone, and didn't fragment and ricochet off to do more damage. They were able to stitch up that nick in a branch of her pulmonary artery and expect her to make a full recovery. I'll have to postpone her return flight to Traverse City, and Sam will have to get along without her for a day or two," Tiny kidded. "But she can get back to the shop before you know it."

"The wedding," Angela whispered weakly.

"And she wants everyone to know that our first Saturday in October double wedding will definitely not be postponed. 'We're getting married in October –r-r,'" Tiny broke out into song again. The nurse standing at the door shushed him with a finger to her lips, but smiled while doing so. Tiny had quickly become a favorite visitor in the ICU ward.

"And don't you worry, Angela," Danny added, "Andrea, Tiny, and I will gladly take your orders in all the planning and arrangements. You won't have to lift a finger except to shake it when we do something wrong."

"You mean like your recent escapade," Tiny glowered at him.

"Hey, big guy, why don't we let Ang rest a bit?" Danny turned again to Angela in her bed and asked, "Okay if I borrow your fiancé for a few minutes? We'll be back soon."

Angela nodded and smiled, glad to put her head back and close her eyes.

Outside in the waiting area, Danny ate his sandwich and filled Tiny in on what had taken place with Buck and Brenda Gibson. But before Tiny could get revved up for yet another assault on his poor judgment, Danny tried to head him off.

"Was it a stupid move? Yeah, I have to admit it, but I think it helped to eliminate Buck and probably the rest of the PUPs from suspicion in Angela's and Mark's shooting."

Tiny listened without much reaction except to shake a giant finger at Danny with a scolding expression on his face. And before he could add words to his admonishing finger shake, Danny was fast to add, "The question is, of course, who else could have done it. And I don't know if it crossed your mind, Tiny, but this was twice in two weeks – and in different parts of the country – that a shooting incident occurred. And I'm the one constant in both occasions. I must be the real target, but why? I seriously doubt any of the PUPs would go that far to try to be rid of a pastor they don't like. Who would want me dead?"

"Really?" Tiny asked in exaggerated animation. "You can't think of anyone who has wanted to 'off' you in the past few years?"

A look of great surprise, disbelief, but sudden awareness struck Danny's face like a roundhouse slap from his powerful friend.

"Sarah? You don't think it could be Sarah? But she's in maximum security with a life sentence. It can't be her."

"Oh," Tiny reacted, leaning back with his arms crossed, "like she's never enlisted anyone else's help in trying to whack you?"

Tiny's probing was like hot needles piercing Danny's mind. Amid the flood of images fighting to terrorize him again from his captivity and almost-murder two and a half years ago, more recent bits of information filtered through into his consciousness. "*Medium height, man in his fifties, gentlemanly in demeanor, soft, Southern-like accent.*"

"Sarah's brother, Ken? Could it be him? Oh, he never seemed like a killer-type. He wouldn't go that far."

Tiny saw that Danny was in denial about the possibility.

"Look, he's a Texan, right? He has a drawl that sounds kinda Southern. Remember that at Sarah's trial here in Pittsburgh he was there, day after day, in the courtroom. You and I both saw him. And he was really shook up about her sentencing. That wasn't any look of fondness and gratitude that he flashed in your direction as they took her away to begin her sentence. I think in his twisted mind and feelings, he may blame you for her imprisonment for the rest of her life, no chance of parole for many years."

Danny mulled over what Tiny was saying in his head.

"It is true," he was forced to admit, "that Sarah said that her big brother Ken was always taking care of her, looking out for her, protecting her. I suppose it's possible that in his aggrieved thinking he wants some sick revenge for her fate."

"And didn't you say that brother Ken was frequently impatient with the slowness of law enforcement procedures and the inefficiency of the justice system. God knows, in my bad, old days I took as much advantage of that as I could."

"You have a point," Danny agreed, starting to come around to Tiny's thinking as a possibility at least, however unlikely it seemed to him. "He had tremendous admiration for the Texas Rangers. He had a friend who was a Ranger and thought that they were more apt to take quick and direct action when it came to law enforcement."

"Well, how can we get a fix on brother Ken's whereabouts and activities? My boys and I can track him down if we know where to start," Tiny suggested.

"I certainly don't know myself," Danny was forced to admit, "but I think I know who might."

Just at that point, Andrea called back to report her flight schedule. She managed to get a plane out of Cherry Capital Airport in Traverse City already Sunday morning, and would arrive at Pittsburgh International that evening, after a lay-over in Detroit. In the meantime, he had worship services to lead at his church while she was in flight.

Danny was excited about her coming. Early Sunday evening they would be reunited with Tiny and Angela, then Monday morning arrange a trip to the State Correctional Facility for women in Muncy, Pennsylvania.

CHAPTER THIRTY-FIVE

Andrea's plane arrived as scheduled Sunday evening. Danny and she hugged and kissed as she came out of the gates area. Tiny had stayed at the hospital with Angela. From her radiant smile and sparkling eyes, Danny knew that Andrea's righteous anger had at least subsided. After their initial "love you's," Andrea spoke up as they headed to pick up her one checked bag from baggage claim.

"You really scared me, Daniel. If anything had happened to you...if those people had set up an ambush...well, words couldn't suffice to express how I would have felt. I can't even think about what it would be like to lose you."

Danny continued to feel torn, pulled in one direction by being glad he had the confrontation with the Gibson's, but pulled hard in the other direction by the pain and concern he had caused people who really cared about him, especially Andrea's love.

"I really am sorry," he replied. "I can't contemplate what it would be like to lose you, either, although I know there's always risk involved in being a law enforcement professional."

"Fair enough," Andrea answered, "but a big difference is

that *we* don't go looking to put ourselves in dangerous situations. And when we do have to face them, we have the best training possible and all of our prior experience to guide us in handling them. Have any courses in seminary on showdowns with murder suspects, or interrogation techniques?"

"Point taken," he admitted. "Speaking of which, I'm really glad you're here now. I have someone I want you to meet, and maybe you can help me find out from her what's really going on with these shootings. Tiny and I think that Sarah might be behind all this."

He proceeded to tell her about the conversation Tiny and he had in the hospital waiting room, and how he intended to go as soon as possible to visit Sarah at the correctional facility in Muncy. Andrea, like just about all police and sheriff's officers in the Grand Traverse area, had heard about Danny's captivity and the intended murder on the part of Sarah and her young lover, Father Frank Lewis. It was one of the more spectacular police incidents in recent years for that normally peaceful region. In one of their times together back in Traverse City, Danny had told her more details about what had happened, so Andrea was fully informed about Sarah and her sick, twisted hate. It would be a challenge, actually meeting and talking with her...if she was willing to be visited.

"Well, this time you're taking me along," she declared without possibility of contradiction. "We're in this together. You might remember, Danny, *I*, too, was almost struck by that bullet at the Cedar Club. You may have been the real target, but I have a very personal stake in what is going on here."

"I want you to go with me," he assured her. He grinned, "I'm glad to have two protectors watching out for me," thinking of both Tiny and Andrea, but not thinking at the time of the most important and effective one - God's Angel of

Providence and Protection.

"Well," Andrea continued to be serious in the face of his trying to make lighter of the discussion, "you certainly shouldn't have to worry about any physical danger in the visitor's room at the correctional facility. But maybe I can help you get some read on what this woman is thinking and saying, assuming she's willing to have me there, too."

Finally, Andrea's checked bag was spit out by the conveyor belt, whisked around on the carousel to where Danny could grab it, and they went to short-term parking to retrieve his Jeep. Andrea naturally wanted to go to the Shadyside Hospital before it got any later and visiting hours would be over. There was no need to check into a hotel. She would be staying at Danny's comfortable South Hills home, and there definitely wouldn't be any reason to clutter up his seldom-used guest room.

The reunion of the four in Angela's room in ICU was crowded, and in violation of the posted limit of only two visitors at a time, but Danny had used his influence as a pastor to bend the rules for a little while. After all, visitor's hours were almost over, and this was a dear friend who had just flown in from Northern Michigan. The four engaged friends hugged and laughed, and some tears of joy and thanksgiving flowed.

Tiny had secured a room in a motel that catered to hospital visitors right next to the hospital, so he went there to spend the night. Danny and Andrea drove down to his house. It was getting late by the time they arrived. He carried her bag up to his bedroom, but then they drew up stools and sat down at his kitchen island with a couple of fast-brewed cups of decaf.

"I'll call the prison at Muncy right away tomorrow morning," Danny said.

Andrea offered in reply, "You might let me talk to them,

too. I can present my credentials as a visiting state police officer from Michigan. And I can legitimately say that I'm following up on a serious crime that occurred two and a half years ago in my jurisdiction, with their inmate as a perpetrator. If they don't bother to look into it too thoroughly, they won't pick up on the fact that the state police didn't have the primary jurisdiction."

"But will the warden's office check on whether you have orders or an active case back in Michigan regarding Sarah Brand?" Danny wondered.

"I'll call my lieutenant first," Andrea suggested. "I think he'd be willing to back me up and say that the Michigan State Police is gathering information so that the state attorney general's office can proceed with prosecution on her kidnapping and attempted murder of you. That way they can go after her if she's ever released from incarceration here in Pennsylvania."

"Good idea. Her release may be pretty unlikely, however. The Allegheny County District Attorney wanted to go for the death penalty for her. Her murder of her husband, the Rev. Dr. William Brand, was a high-profile case involving the death of a prominent citizen. It was clearly premeditated, and she certainly didn't display any remorse. It was probably only her substantial wealth, enabling her to hire some of the best defense attorneys in Pittsburgh, that enabled her to dodge incarceration on death row. They pleaded it as a crime of passion, with expert witnesses testifying to her diminished capacity, and played on the sympathy of some of the jurors by claiming that she was the victim of domestic abuse, especially psychological and emotional abuse since she had never filed a police report documenting physical abuse."

"Nonetheless," Andrea countered, "the State of Michigan and the County of Leelanau deferred to Pennsylvania since the only murder she actually committed occurred here, but the case against her back in Michigan can still be prosecuted should Pennsylvania ever grant her freedom. I'll make that call in the morning."

CHAPTER THIRTY-SIX

Andrea was right; her lieutenant, the Post Commander, said he'd vouch for her should the warden's office contact him. He wished her good luck with their attempt to get information from Sarah and admonished her to limit her involvement and by all means, to be careful and stay safe.

Danny then called the Warden's Office at the correctional facility in Muncy. He asked for permission to visit Sarah Brand and then put Andrea on the phone. She explained who she was, that she was accompanying Dr. Henriks for this visit to the prison, and the reason for her involvement. The administrative assistant transferred their call to the warden herself, who was very cooperative, replied that she would see to it that Sarah Brand was available to meet with them, and that very afternoon would be fine.

"Well, that was easy enough," Danny said with relief. "We can get underway by 10:00. It's about a four hours' drive by highway, so we can stop for a quick bite to eat around State College, and then drive on to Williamsburg. Muncy is less than a half hour further east, so we should make it by 2:30-3:00."

"We'll divide up the driving," Andrea insisted. "And just

so you know, I checked my personal sidearm in my bag at the airport. Since I'm not really assigned on a case, it wouldn't have been correct procedure to pack my service pistol, but the little P238 Sig Sauer that fits in my ankle holster can do the job just fine, and let's not forget, there's still someone out there who's gunning for you. He's tried twice now, and we're not about to have third time be the charm."

CHAPTER THIRTY-SEVEN

Danny was exactly precise, as usual, about their schedule for their trip to Muncy. They arrived at the correctional facility without any difficulty at about 2:45. Their visit was in the prison's schedule for the day and they were easily checked in. Andrea handed over her .380 caliber sidearm and by shortly after 3:00 they were seated in the visitor's room on one side of a bare table.

They hadn't been there for more than a few minutes when a guard came through the door opposite them, accompanied by Sarah Brand in restraints. As a convicted murderer, she was considered dangerous, and had, in fact, been in more than one violent altercation among fellow prisoners. The guard seated her opposite Danny and Andrea and then stepped back several feet, but stayed in the room, her eyes on Sarah most of the time.

Before any words were exchanged, Danny noticed how different Sarah appeared and acted. As soon as she was brought into the room, he noticed that her previously long hair had been cropped short. Sarah had found that prison fights with her fellow inmates typically included hair-pulling and that it was to her advantage to wear her graying hair short. She looked harder and tougher, with deepened lines around her eyes and mouth, and eyes that squinted in the bright light of the room. She didn't seem surprised to see him since she had surely been informed that he was coming.

"Well, Daniel Henriks, I never expected to see you again...nor can I say I wanted to," she began their conversation. "And who's this little chippy you have with you?" – using a deliberately offensive term for a promiscuous woman or a prostitute.

Neither Danny nor Andrea reacted to her slur, both maintaining their professional composure. Danny answered, however.

"This is Officer Andrea Wilkins of the Michigan State Police. She also happens to be my fiancée."

"Oh, that's rich," Sarah laughed derisively. "First you reject me and all that money we could have enjoyed, then you hitch up with a civil servant. Well at least she doesn't look that bad. How's she in bed?"

"None of your business, Sarah," Danny shut her off. "You can hold your tongue. We have some questions for you."

"Oh, skip the small talk and get right down to business, eh? Well, the warden said she was requiring me to meet with you, but that doesn't mean I have to answer any questions."

Danny and Andrea had decided on the ride there that they would try a direct assault and see if they could catch her off-guard. So, Danny countered with "Even if they have to do with what happened to your dear brother Ken?"

"What about Ken? What do you mean what happened to him?"

He had clearly struck some nerve. Sarah was used to acting by now as though she didn't care much about life outside the prison walls, but he was right. Whether there was anything or anyone else, she cared very much about Ken, her loyal older brother.

Taking a deliberate gamble, Andrea inserted, "We're investigating Kenneth Romano's involvement in two recent shootings, with one fatality. What do you know about his whereabouts and his actions?"

The reaction on Sarah's part was slight and subtle, but discernible to both Andrea and Danny. She visibly flinched just a little, obviously surprised that they had tied together Ken and the shootings.

"I don't know what you're talking about. Kenny wouldn't shoot anybody. You're barking up a wrong tree." She leaned back and acted more confident, but Danny and Andrea thought they had shaken her a bit.

The warden had confirmed for them that a male relative had visited Sarah several times in the recent past, so Danny pressed her harder.

"Cut the act, Sarah, we know that Ken's been here to see you, and that the two of you have conspired to try once again to kill me. I don't care one little bit about your hatred of me, but you should help Ken before the police dragnet tightens around him and he comes to a violent end."

"Help us, so that we can help him," Andrea added, "there's been more than enough bloodshed, don't let it be his."

***

Even in her imprisonment, Sarah had been hard-put to modify her expectations of having things always go her way. She had, in fact, conspired with Ken and egged him on to finish her attempt to get rid of Danny, but she never thought so far as to appreciate the danger their planning was creating for Ken. She just wanted her revenge. But now her eyes darted a bit from one side to the other, as though she was trying to think about what she should say and do...for Ken's sake. For the moment at least, she decided to try to dodge their pressure.

"Sure, Kenny's been here to see me. He's my brother, after all, but I don't know where he is now. Probably gone back home to Texas. You might check down there in his Houston suburb."

Sarah had always been good at planning in meticulous detail her future actions, but she had never been very good when put on the spot and having to come up with immediate reactions. Danny kept after her.

"You know he isn't down there, Sarah, we've gone by his motel, and he hasn't checked out yet, so he still intends to hang around and be back to see you. Where is he now?" It was a bold lie, but it worked well enough to open a crack in her tough shell.

"You've been to the Sunset?" she blurted in surprise that they would know he had a motel room near the prison. "Oh, don't hurt him. He and Sally are all I have left, and I don't know..." She caught herself, realizing that she had just said too much.

Angry at her slip, and at their pressuring her, she instantly became belligerent, pushed back from the table and called for the guard.

"Guard, we're done here. Take me back." And the guard took her from the room, but not before Sarah shot a murderous glance back at Danny, infuriated that they had tripped her up.

Back in Danny's Grand Cherokee, Andrea said, "Well, I'd say she was a bit too quick to suggest that we look for her brother in Houston."

Danny nodded in agreement and said, "Yes. It was a rather weak attempt at spontaneous deflection."

As Danny drove out of the prison complex, Andrea smiled

at him and said, "I guess I know where we're headed now." And she reached down and checked the holster for her Sig Sauer, making sure that it was ready for quick release.

"Yup, straight to the Sunset Motel," he answered with a determined look on his face.

CHAPTER THIRTY-EIGHT

"We should call the Lycoming County Sheriff's Department and let them know there may be a murder suspect at the Sunset Motel outside Muncy," Andrea asserted.

"I agree," Danny replied. "But don't you think Sarah would have gotten to a phone as soon as she left the visitor's room? I remember passing the place on the way in here; it's right off Interstate 180, by the exit. If you support me on this, I think we should find out if he really does still have a room there. Maybe we can at least keep watch until the sheriff deputies get there, and see if he takes off and what direction he goes in."

"Okay," Andrea agreed reluctantly, "but I'm calling them now, and you and I are not going to confront him if he's still there. He still has a high-powered .308, you know."

In just a few minutes they reached the motel. Andrea quickly perused the cars in the lot.

"No Texas plates. I didn't think he'd actually use his own car. Why don't I go in and check with the motel manager?" Andrea suggested. "You stay out here and keep watch, both for any signs of Ken, you know what he looks like, and for the sheriff deputies. And for God's sake and mine, don't even think of approaching him if you spot him. Stay in the car and speed dial me if he shows up, but don't do anything stupid."

Her orders were definite and without wiggle room. All Danny could say was "Yes, ma'am."

Within a couple of minutes, Andrea returned from the motel office.

"We're too late. We probably hadn't gotten out of the correctional facility before a 'Tom Butler' checked out of the motel and took off."

"Tom Butler? He used a fake ID?"

"For purposes of checking into the motel, yes, it seems that way. The motel manager gave the right description: average height, about 190 lbs, graying hair, spoke with a Southern/Texan accent."

"What about his car," Danny wondered. "Did he have a description of that...license plate number...anything?"

"As motels do," Andrea replied, "the check-in card had a make, model, and a Pennsylvania license number, which I wrote down, but the clerk certainly didn't go out in the parking lot to verify the information. Ken could have put down fictitious information, used a rental car, or even had an extra set of plates in the trunk to switch on and off. I'll give the information to the highway patrol when they show up here, but I really doubt that it will help. He could be anywhere by now, and his vehicle may not be anything like what the motel had."

Danny mulled over what Andrea told him. "Sarah must have been able to call him as soon as the guard took her away from us."

"Or," she offered, "he may even have been keeping surveillance on us as we entered and left the prison. He certainly knows what your Grand Cherokee looks like. We need to maintain hyper-vigilance. If he's really obsessed with doing you in out of revenge for his baby sister, it's possible he hasn't really left, but could be watching and taking aim right now."

That thought made Danny slump in his driver's seat and look around futilely. He didn't want to present Ken with a target a third time. Maybe his aim would finally improve. But just then a sheriff's patrol car drove up, and Andrea got out to speak to the deputies and to share with them what information she had gathered. Danny wasn't going to hide and cower in his Jeep, but he exited the driver's side door slowly, continuing to look around for any possible threat. He kept back a few feet as Andrea continued to talk to the officers, and he continued to swivel his head around, scanning the nearby woods for any movement.

Andrea finally turned around and walked the few steps back to Danny.

"They'll put out a BOLO on a vehicle based on this description to all law enforcement agencies in this area, but I have to tell you, I don't think what we have is accurate. He may not even be using the same vehicle that was at the Seven-Eleven last Saturday at the time of the shooting."

"If so, then he must have slipped away just in time," Danny said glumly.

"I'm afraid so," Andrea agreed, "and we still have to regard him as a dangerous threat. He may even become more desperate to get you, now that he knows we're on to him. We have to be prepared for the possibility that he could try again at any time, in any location. I'm not leaving your side, Buster, until he's caught, you're safe, and this is all over. Think of me as your permanent appendage, with my .380 always within reach."

"Sounds like my fondest dream," Danny smiled, trying to make at least a little lighter of the situation. But Andrea wasn't in the mood for even her famous smile. She continued to be completely serious and authoritative in tone. "Come on, let's get out of here."

CHAPTER THIRTY-NINE

At that very moment, Kenneth Romano was driving east on a secondary road, State Highway 405. Heading not back toward Pittsburgh, and definitely not south and west in the general direction of Texas, he would stay off the interstates, follow State Highway 118, and actually make his way up to Scranton. For one thing, nobody would expect him to head in that direction. For another thing, he had called ahead to the Wilkes-Barre/Scranton International Airport, used a second false ID that he had saved as a back-up, and booked a flight to Detroit, Michigan.

He knew that things would be too hot for him back in Pittsburgh. Danny Henriks' detective sergeant friend and his CSI investigators would surely have gathered evidence, tracks, witness descriptions, his brass casing and the bullet from his fatal shot. And, they would have alerted all law enforcement agencies to be on the lookout, including at the airports in the area. If he returned there for yet another attempt at that accursed Rev. Dr. Henriks, he could well be snatched up long before he got in range for a third shot.

And there certainly wasn't any reason to head back to Houston or anywhere else in Texas. As the case against his dear sister had developed, her arraignment held, pre-trial motions made, trial date finally set, jury selected...on and on the legal process ground for weeks and months. Ken had been there for all of it, agonizing as Sarah was dragged through the excruciating procedures. Every day had been heart-breaking for him. Eventually he filed for early retirement from his Houston-based company.

He had accumulated a substantial amount in employee stock purchases and kept building his 401(k) and overall investment portfolio. He had kept adding to his investments, never taking any withdrawals, and had gotten to the point where he really didn't have to keep working anymore. He could live off his investment income.

His total commitment to be there for Sarah had put tremendous strain on his marriage and family. His wife and children couldn't understand how he could be so supportive of his sister when she was frankly a calculating, cold-blooded murderer of her famous husband. Her guilt wasn't in question, and it had been compounded by her efforts to hold Danny captive and murder not only him, but her lover, Frank, also. Ken's wife and kids had tried to talk sense into him, to convince him that, okay, he didn't have to stop loving her, but neither did he have to dedicate all his days, weeks, and months to little else but sitting in the courtroom, neglecting all of them just to moan and gnash his teeth over his sick sibling.

His wife had been opposed to his early retirement and his seemingly never-ending vigil in Pittsburgh, and while she initially spent some weeks there with him, finally she gave him an ultimatum. She wanted him to come home to Houston and rejoin the family he belonged to there. But in his obsession, it was as though he could hardly even hear what she had to say.

"But I can't leave Sarah. She was driven to do what she

did. She didn't really have a choice. They should hospitalize her, not imprison her." He would say over and over again. "You heard the experts; she didn't really know what she was doing. She was abused by that Bill Brand and acted in self-defense. And damn that Daniel Henriks for treating her the way he did. And he's free and she's rotting in prison." And he would get so worked up that he literally ground his teeth together in frustration and anger. The trial arguments had just cemented his rage firmly in his head, and there was no talking to him about the facts of the whole affair.

After about six months, his wife filed for legal separation. She remained in their Houston suburban home since he had no interest in returning to it, and he continued to stay in long-term residential housing near the Allegheny County Courthouse. After her conviction and, finally, her sentencing and transfer to the correctional facility in Muncy, he followed and made arrangements for yet more long-term motel accommodations. His world had shrunk so drastically that he didn't seem to mind living by himself in such limited conditions, visiting Sarah in prison two or three times a week for going on two years now. But that despicable Daniel Henriks had just ruined that, too.

It was entirely justifiable in Ken's twisted mind that Sarah and he surreptitiously began to concoct a plan to try again to murder Danny. He had deserved to die at her hand, but failing that, her totally devoted brother would finish the job for her. He first learned that Danny and his slum-ghetto friend were going to take a week's vacation up in Northern Michigan, very near Sarah's old summer home in Leelanau County. Ken had learned the area well, especially since he had spent time there, arranging the listing and sale of the lovely "cottage." It just wasn't right that Sarah had lost that, too. That Sunday afternoon he had almost succeeded at the Cedar gun range. In fact, he could scarcely believe that he missed. His aim had been precise.

Admittedly, his second attempt at the abomination of a wedding was trickier. The trajectory of the shot was quite steeply downhill, requiring him to aim a bit high to compensate, but he had almost succeeded. He would not fail a third time. But first he had to make his escape out of Pennsylvania. The entire sixty-seven miles he fumed and smoldered as he obsessed over the entire last two and a half years of Sarah's pain and suffering...as well as his own. But he had been right. Nobody had an actual description of the car he had rented for months at a time. His old Lexus sedan remained at his old home in Houston. He had, in fact, thought to steal license plates off another car in a mall parking lot one night, and he switched them for the rental company's plates, just in case anyone *had* taken down a plate number at the Seven-Eleven. Then when he drove off from there, he found an opportunity to put the rental company's plates back on. No one pulled him over along route 118.

He pulled into the rental car company's lot at the airport, dropped the keys in the night box, and caught an airport shuttle to the terminal. His fake photo ID matched his appearance, of course, and he picked up his ticket at the counter. He had just one large duffle with him, and his case with his laptop. The .308 rifle he had dropped, with the ammunition, into the Susquehanna River when he came to it, making sure that he could do so unobserved. It wouldn't be that hard to replace it at one of the many gun shows during the month of September in a hunting and shooting state like Michigan.

The flight to Detroit was uneventful. Ken leaned back in the first-class seat and closed his eyes. He thought about his still-unfulfilled goal. He had learned that Danny had a new love interest. *How could he so callously reject a rich and beautiful woman like Sarah and later take up with a bitch cop in Northern Michigan?* She had first appeared to him in his rifle scope when she stood next to Danny at the end of the sporting clays course. Most recently she had even accompanied him at the prison when he confronted Sarah.

Ken managed to find out more simply by calling the South Presbyterian Church office the Friday before the homosexual wedding. In the conversation with Mildred, the church secretary, he had posed as a guest planning to attend the wedding and wanting to check on the schedule for the wedding service, the reception, and whether there was a place to drop off gifts. As Mildred and he chit-chatted, he dropped the item that he had heard Dr. Henriks had a new fiancée himself.

"Oh, yes," Mildred gleefully shared, "we're so excited for him. They've already set a date for the first Saturday in October. It's awfully quick, and the wedding won't even be here at his church. They're being married at her Presbyterian Church in Traverse City, Michigan. And it's going to be a double wedding. They're getting married in a joint service with his good friend and his fiancée. Can you imagine that?"

"That *is* remarkable," Ken agreed; "I certainly hope he thinks to invite me to that wedding, too."

"I'll be sure to leave a message for him that you called, Mr.......?"

"No need," Ken stopped her politely. "I'll just speak to him in person at Tim and Mark's wedding. Thank you so much for your help."

Since it was now mid-September, Ken would have to lay low, be patient, and wait a couple of weeks, but the first Saturday in October sounded like a fine time to crash another wedding. He would have plenty of time to make plans and preparations since he would be in Michigan again well in advance of Danny's return. He would case the layout of the church, the entrances and exits, the best way to get away after he fulfilled his mission, the best alternative if a sudden change of plans was necessary.

Ken thought hard about what had gone wrong in his first two attempts. He had felt confident with the accurate .308 Remington 700 rifle, even enjoying the idea of striking Henriks down from a comfortable distance, but now he felt as though there were too many variables that could affect his shot. And part of the challenge at the homosexual wedding was trying to get a clear shot at Danny in his pulpit robe with all those other people milling around in front of the church. He had to be more certain on this third opportunity. Perhaps it was time to go to a handgun, to create a circumstance where Danny would be alone, or just with his girlfriend, and Ken could make it much more "up close and personal." Yes, he liked that idea....to be able to look into the eyes of his victim and tell him, "This is for Sarah."

But if the girlfriend was present, Ken would have to deal with her, too. And she *was* a well-trained law enforcement professional, maybe not like a Texas Ranger, but not to be taken too lightly. She surely wouldn't be packing under her wedding dress...but no, Ken didn't want to try to deal with the crowd of people that would be present, especially Danny's huge friend. He'd give it some careful thought, keep tight surveillance during the few days prior to their wedding, figure out the best opportunity. But he would not be denied again, no, sir. Daniel Henriks was one of the walking dead.

It was late when his plane touched down at Detroit Metro, but he easily found his duffle at baggage claim, walked out to the rental car lot, chose an available car, ready and waiting for him, and drove off into the night, heading north on I-75. He would disappear in the North Woods until it was time. And Sarah would understand that he had gone underground. He couldn't risk contacting her; they would surely be monitoring any communications she received or made. But the day would come when sister and brother could celebrate together that her revenge was complete...and that would give him rest at last.

CHAPTER FORTY

Tuesday morning found Danny and Andrea relaxing over breakfast at his kitchen table. They agreed that they had lots of questions with few answers, except that it had now become clear that Sarah Brand's older brother, Ken Romano, was the shooter both at the Cedar Rod & Gun Club in Leelanau County, Michigan, and at Mark and Tim's wedding at South Presbyterian Church in Pittsburgh, Pennsylvania. It was Ken who was gunning for Danny, seeking bizarre revenge for the life sentence and incarceration of Sarah.

Among the things they didn't know:

1) Whether the Leelanau County Sheriff's Department had gotten helpful information out of Wes Smith or other evidence to identify adequately the shooter there.
2) Whether Detective Sergeant Jim Bradley and his investigative crew had sufficient evidence to make the case against Ken in an Allegheny County Court.
3) What, if anything, the police had done with Buck and Brenda Gibson.
4) What had happened with the Lycoming County

Sheriff's BOLO and search for a fleeing Ken Romano.

5) And obviously, just where Ken was now, what was he planning, and how and when might he attempt yet a third shooting?

Multiple law enforcement agencies in different states were involved in trying to make a case against Ken and track him down for an arrest, but at this point it seemed to Danny and Andrea that he had disappeared. For all they knew, he could have set up a sniper's nest right outside Danny's South Hills, Pittsburgh, home. Andrea was 100% right. Hyper-vigilance and extreme caution were essential for them until Ken was finally apprehended. She would keep her Sig Sauer on her at all times.

"You know," Danny put it to her as she sipped her coffee, "I still have a concealed carry permit for my Ruger. I can go out armed, too."

Andrea frowned. "I respect your shooting ability, love, and know you want to protect me, but I'm not entirely comfortable with you packing, too. With me, it's a matter of an off-duty police officer permitted to carry a personal sidearm, and I *am* trained in responding to unforeseen situations that might require the drawing of my weapon in response to a legitimate threat. Have you run multiple scenarios in the training course at a police shooting range?"

Not wanting Danny to feel put down, she added with a sheepish grin, "My first few times, I accidentally shot pop-up targets of a woman carrying grocery bags in both arms, a homeless man in an alley holding not a gun but a bottle, and worst, a little girl who jumped up from behind her bed with a teddy bear in her arms. Got her and the bear, too."

Danny laughed, but had to agree; he wasn't trained in shooting much other than paper and clay targets, despite his confidence when confronting the Gibson's.

"You're right," he reluctantly deferred to Andrea's judgment. "But I'm going to keep it handy, anyway. If Ken Romano goes so far as to break into my home while we're here, I want to have it within reach. Whatever comes our way, we're a team, and we'll deal with it together."

"I know," she hugged him and held him tightly. "I wouldn't have it any other way."

Had they both realized it, they could have relaxed and put away any and all weaponry. Not only was Ken far away, but the Angel of Providence and Protection kept his home as safe as anywhere could be outside the Kingdom of Heaven.

CHAPTER FORTY-ONE

Among all the things Danny and Andrea didn't know, what concerned them the most was how Angela and Tiny were doing, what her recovery was looking like, or what her long-term prognosis was determined to be. They felt greatly encouraged for her but wondered if she would suffer any lingering effects from her wounding. They agreed that Danny would check in with Mildred in the church office as it was now open for the day, deal with any immediate questions or issues, and then the two of them would head back to Shadyside Hospital to see Angela and Tiny.

Angela was still in ICU, but the tube draining blood and fluid from her lung was helping greatly to restore her breathing capacity. She looked stronger and managed a soft "Hi, guys" when they entered. Tiny was eager to give them an update.

"The doc was in already this morning, and he gave us a good report. The suturing is holding; the lung is clearing; she can get up for limited minutes, and she should be out of intensive care by the end of this week."

"She'll go to a regular hospital room then?" Andrea asked.

"Yes, but if she continues to do well, with no relapses,"

Tiny smiled, "by the end of the following week we hope she can be sent home with me."

"What about long-term prognosis?" Danny wondered.

"She'll be ambulatory when she's in the regular room?" Andrea assumed.

"Yup," Tiny confirmed. "With moderate exercise once out of this place, but maybe six weeks total before she can get back to work and all her favorite activities...oh, say, about the middle of, or three weeks into, October."

"You know," Danny suggested, "our double wedding is scheduled for about two weeks before her getting back to a normal schedule. Maybe we could postpone our date?"

Andrea looked at Angela and nodded her okay, but Angela motioned for Tiny and the two of them to lean closer to her. As they did so, in definitely the strongest voice Tiny had heard since her surgery, Angela declared, "I said it before: the wedding's on. I'll be there if big boy here has to carry me to the altar."

Tiny beamed, "And I would do it, no problem." And the four of them hugged and there were smiles and tears of rejoicing.

Andrea and Danny left the hospital and reviewed how things stood for them as they drove to South Presbyterian Church. Among other things that needed his attention, Danny had to talk with Mildred about Mark's memorial service. Tim and Mark's family had conferred Monday and decided that rather than a full funeral service, they preferred to have a family and close friends memorial service with a closed casket Friday morning at 11:00, followed by interment at Lakewood Memorial Gardens. Then they would have an early afternoon lunch back at the church.

A lot of the details and arrangements at the church could be handled by Mildred. Danny would prepare a funeral message emphasizing the celebration of Mark's life and the surety of his hope for a resurrection to eternal life with Christ the Lord. Opportunity would be given for at least a few of those attending to share loving memories of Mark. Tim himself could speak to their mutual love, and the joy they felt in being married, but Danny would keep things open and flexible if Tim didn't feel able to speak when the time came.

Tuesday evening Danny would meet with Tim and Mark's parents to plan the service and provide his pastoral care, support, and prayers. Tim left a note at the church office stating that in lieu of flowers, he wanted any monetary gifts to go to More Light Presbyterians, a coalition of individuals, local groups, and congregations in the Presbyterian Church, USA. They worked for full inclusion of gay, lesbian, bisexual, transgender, and questioning people of faith in the whole life and faith of Presbyterian churches and all Christian churches. Mildred would inform people who called in about the service about Tim's wishes, as well as put an announcement in the brief service bulletin.

"Well, while I never had the chance to meet Mark," Andrea said, "from what you've told me, that sounds like a great way to memorialize his life and honor his marriage to Tim."

"It is," Danny agreed. "Also, I've told Tim that the Personnel Committee and I support his taking whatever time off he needs – to grieve, to spend time with his own family and Mark's, even to give of his time and efforts to More Light and whatever other groups he may want to. He said that he was most grateful and that he would think about that and let me know of his decision at Friday's service and lunch."

"Which reminds me," Andrea spoke up, "after we stop for lunch in a few minutes, I need to call my lieutenant and let him know more precisely just when I will be back to work. I know I said that I would be your appendage and not leave your side until Ken was apprehended and an end put to

Sarah's and his attempts on your life, but if I want to keep my job and help support us once *we're* married, I'm afraid I need to get back to Traverse City at the end of this week. Hope that's okay," she looked at him entreatingly.

"Of course," Danny encouraged her. "I promise, really promise, that I'll be vigilant, cautious, and stay as safe as possible by all the standards of heaven and earth."

"And no more 'cowboy' stuff," she ordered in no uncertain terms. "No solo meetings with him or anybody who could be allied with him, no waltzing into potential ambushes, no taking chances of any kind."

"I promise," he repeated. "Nothing that would paint a target on my back...or front," he smiled.

Andrea was not amused. "I mean it, Buster. I'm only leaving you on your own here if you make a sacred vow not to endanger yourself and our future life together."

"As God is my witness," Danny said with great solemnity. But Danny being Danny, he couldn't help smiling and adding, "And I have a whole stack of Bibles I can swear on."

Andrea was still not amused. "I don't care whether you swear on your stack of Bibles or your dear mother's grave; you just keep yourself safe. I love you."

"I love you, too," he assured her. "More than anything."

CHAPTER FORTY-TWO

The rest of the week went quickly. Mark's memorial service was held on Friday morning with about 25 people in attendance, including Andrea and Tiny, who had left Angela's side for the first time since her shooting only because her strong recovery enabled her planned transfer to a regular hospital room early that morning. She told him to go to the service and that he needed to represent the two of them and express deepest condolences to Tim.

At the post-interment lunch Tim announced his decision about time off to Danny.

"I've been grateful," he said, "for this week off. And I'm especially grateful for the service you conducted this morning. It was an uplifting celebration of Mark's life, and even though I was just too choked up to say anything, it meant everything for you and Mark's family and friends to share what a giving person he was. He loved life, he loved all people, and I will never regret that he loved me."

"I know," Danny comforted him, "and we all loved him, too. I'm sorrier than words can express that he was taken from you as soon as you were finally married."

"Nonetheless," Tim declared with a tear in his eye but a

strong voice, "I had him for several years, and I know he agrees with me that we were married in God's sight all that time. Still, it was worth it for both of us to 'tie the knot' as far as the State of Pennsylvania and the Presbyterian Church were concerned," he managed a brave smile.

Changing the subject a bit, Tim went on. "I think I'd really like to get back to work and our ministry here at our church next week. I think that will be better therapy for me than sitting around, looking at Mark's things in our condo. I've already gotten permission from his family to donate his clothes and some of his personal items to the Clothes Closet here at the church for the homeless. What I will keep are his paintings, although I told his parents that they or the rest of his family can choose two or three that they would like to have, and the big, 4' by 4' oil he did of Jesus as the Good Shepherd I'll donate to More Light for their fall benefit dinner and raffle."

"Oh, speaking of More Light," Danny was reminded, "memorial gifts in Mark's name are still coming in to the church office, and I'm sure will continue to do so during this coming week, but the sum is totaling in the thousands now."

"That's just great," Tim reacted with delight and relief. "I was hoping for a good response from all the people whose lives Mark touched."

"And really," Danny went on, "we can get along just fine if you want an additional week off, or even more, perhaps?"

"Thank you, but it's now the very middle of September. Youth groups, Wednesday evening kids' programs, adult study groups, all that and more has just started up for the new fall season, and I want to be there for them. Besides, in less than a couple of weeks you'll be off again for your Northern Michigan fall vacation and wedding. Maybe you should be the one taking additional time. Two weeks isn't much time to get there, be married, have a honeymoon, and get back here. Will it be with a new bride in tow?"

"You wouldn't put it like that if you knew Andrea better. Nobody tows *her* around. But I'll fill you in on those plans another time," Danny responded. "For now, both of us need to spend some time with your family members and guests. First, however, I'm heading back to the dessert table for a second slice of apple pie. Our Women's Association ladies have done themselves proud for you and Mark."

Andrea joined him as he headed for the slices of pie. "We have to stop meeting like this," she kidded. "You're not going to be able to fit into your pulpit robe if you keep having second slices of pie."

"I agree," Danny mumbled with a big bite of apple pie in his mouth, "but just this once?"

She shook her head in mock disgust. They sat down at a table by themselves.

"I'm scheduled for a flight out of Pittsburgh International Airport tomorrow morning at 7:58," Andrea told him. "That will get me back to Cherry Capital in Traverse City by late afternoon, with a bit of a lay-over in Detroit. Not only will that enable me to rest up a bit on Sunday before reporting to the Post Monday morning, but it would be nice to sing with my choir at the Sunday service."

"As much as I hate to have you go," Danny admitted, "that sounds good, and it will only be about a week and a half before Tiny, Angela and I drive up to Traverse City for our wedding. Our plan is to get there Wednesday evening, spend Thursday with wedding preparations, have our rehearsal on Friday evening, and the wedding itself Saturday at 1:30 in the afternoon."

"Okay, we're keeping it all simple but beautiful. My mom and dad will fly up there from Ohio where they live near my younger sister. The rest of my relatives we can visit and share with them later, toward the holidays. You don't have anyone coming to the wedding, so our guest list will be really short, mostly friends and co-workers. Tiny doesn't have anyone, either, and Angela's remaining relatives are in Southern California, which is too far away on such short notice."

"Tim said he would like to be there with us," Danny added, "but I have to have him take care of services and everything else here at South Presbyterian. But all we really need is the four of us, your pastor, and maids of honor. You have yours chosen, right?"

"Yes, I have a best friend at the church who is a fellow choir member, Lucy Johnson, who gleefully accepted my request. Our Post Commander, Lieutenant Wade, offered to walk me down the aisle if my elderly father couldn't make it. I thanked him, but said that we were walking in together, all four of us, with nobody 'giving anyone away' but we ourselves. I believe Angela asked her boss's wife, Julie, to be her matron of honor, since they've worked together at the shop for the last two years and more."

"And Tiny and I agreed that each of us would be 'best man' for the other. He's really my best friend, anyway."

"Perfect," Andrea summed it up, and Danny knew that she meant it as literally as humanly possible. "Now, we've gone over the precautions you need to take not to give Ken a third opportunity to try to shoot you. Nobody seems to know where he went when he left Muncy, or where he is now. The Lycoming County dragnet came up empty, and your sergeant friend Jim has evidence that points to him, but he hasn't surfaced in his old haunts in Texas and has stayed completely away from and out of touch with sister Sarah. So, again, please be careful and watchful every second of every day."

Having become better at discerning when he could make light of things with Andrea and when he should not, Danny replied as seriously as he could, "And I'll stay away from uncovered windows both at work and at home, always check my car for any tampering or an unwanted occupant in hiding, survey my surroundings as soon as I arrive wherever I'm going, and especially stay away from the Keystone shooting ranges or anywhere else people are freely brandishing guns. Plus, as Tiny scales back on his 24/7 vigil with our recovering Angela, I'll have the protection services of him and his 'boys.'"

"Good." Angela pronounced. "Let's just get you through the next couple of weeks, and after that I'll keep you safe myself, as though we're joined at the hip."

"Hip to hip, hey, I like that...and other full body contact," he smiled and winked as Andrea giggled. But then Danny turned serious again. "Don't you forget, my love, that you, too, need to maintain watchfulness and precautions. He knows who you are now, and as twisted as he has to be, there's no way of knowing if he might try to strike at me through you. And I'm much more fearful of him hurting you than anything he could do to me. Although there's no indication that he might have returned to Michigan."

"I'm totally mindful of the possible danger to me." Andrea assured him. "I won't let my guard down for a second, and while I will have my service weapon with me when I'm working, as I said before, the Sig Sauer is with me at all times." And she pointed down to the slight bump near the ankle of her right pant leg.

"I knew there was a reason you were always wearing jeans, khakis, and pant suits this week," Danny replied. "And well-accessorized, too." Both laughed and hugged each other.

CHAPTER FORTY-THREE

Ken Romano had arrived back in Northern Michigan and carefully considered where he could lie low and not draw anyone's attention, especially any branch of law enforcement. He decided against his usual use of long-term motels, since after his stay at the Sunset outside Muncy, motels might be the first places authorities would look for him. He certainly didn't want to return to Leelanau County at this point. For one thing, he had no idea if the sheriff's department there was still on the lookout for him, and for another thing, the Leelanau Peninsula highways were too easy to seal off if an active manhunt got underway to capture him.

He stopped by the Buckley Country Store on Highway 37, filled the gas tank of his rental car. He saw a large bulletin board cluttered with people's business cards and photos of things for sale, from used fishing boats to kittens and puppies, and announcements of upcoming area events, including a few that were long past. The store employees seldom bothered with keeping up with bulletin boards because it was a hassle and extra work. Some handwritten announcements advertising "room for rent" caught his eye.

There, one of those might do well, he thought, as he took down a couple of them. The first one he checked out was at an old farmhouse on an unpaved county road back in the woods outside Buckley, more or less on the way to Traverse City. The elderly, widowed owner lived alone and when Ken went to see the room and meet her, she was quite glad that someone could rent the upstairs spare bedroom. It would give her a little income, and that "the old place won't seem so empty now," she smiled.

"Well, I'm delighted I can use it for a few months," Ken replied, "while I work construction up in Traverse City. It will be much quieter and more peaceful than staying in a busy motel up there. And while I'm here, perhaps I can give a hand occasionally – bring in some firewood for your wood stove with winter soon approaching, or maybe you'd like some leaves raked?"

My, what a nice man this John Jacobs is – the name on Ken's false driver's license that none of the authorities were aware of – the elderly woman thought, a *charming, gentleman. A bit of an accent, I wonder where he's from originally,* she thought, but didn't ask because she didn't want to seem too nosy or invade his privacy. *Everybody's so-o concerned about privacy these days. In my day we just said "None of your business" if we wanted to be private. Well, it'll be nice to have him here.*

Ken settled into his new accommodations, which included a private bath room in the upstairs hall and kitchen privileges. He decided that he would mostly keep to himself, but he would leave every morning as if he was going to that fictitious construction job in Traverse City. It would be a good idea if he drove around and thoroughly familiarized himself with the Grand Traverse area.

The following week on Wednesday Ken took a drive up to Traverse City in the morning. He had deliberately stayed away from the Presbyterian Church where Danny and his group would have their wedding so as not to attract anyone's attention, but he decided that now it was time to scout out the church and plan his third, finally successful, attempt on Danny's life.

Before doing anything else, he parked across the street from the church in the public parking lot. No one would pay any attention to a car with Michigan plates, whose driver was presumably in the nearby office building. Then, he strolled nonchalantly up the street, turned left at the cross street and walked down to the far entrance in the back of the church parking lot. There he was virtually unnoticeable by anyone leaving the main doors of the church. He counted the various doors in and out of the church building. There were three that he could see from that vantage point. He continued to stroll as if he was merely someone out for an afternoon walk. On the opposite side of the church there were seven more doors at different points, including a service door.

Ken crossed the street back to his car. *There are too many doors*, he decided. If he tried to confront Danny and shoot him in the church itself, there were too many escape points if he missed initially. He had already ruled out taking his shot during the wedding activities that first Saturday in October but had thought perhaps he could ambush Danny the Friday night before while he was at the rehearsal. But the more he thought of it, the more he felt that he still didn't want to deal with the group that would be at the rehearsal.

His best opportunity, he concluded, was to lie in wait near the parking lot of the church, perhaps spring his ambush as soon as Danny exited his Grand Cherokee to go into the church for the rehearsal. His fiancée would undoubtedly be in the passenger seat, and if Ken struck quickly, he could shoot Danny down before he went around to open the door for the woman. There was undoubtedly a good chance that his big friend would be in the back seat, but his attention would undoubtedly be on *his* fiancée. Surprise and striking quickly would be essential. He would be aided, however, by the fact that the October sun would have already gone down, and the parking lot would be well-shadowed, since he had called and learned that the rehearsal was at 7:30 p.m.

Ken decided that he would watch carefully as Danny's Jeep pulled slowly into the parking lot. He should park in the center section, closest to the main doors of the church. Ken would park his car earlier, taking the first stall that wasn't reserved for handicapped parking. That would compel Danny to park on the other side of him from the church. He'd slouch over on the passenger side so that he wasn't seen, open the door quickly as soon as he saw Danny getting out, and shoot before he even closed his car door.

The one variable would be if Danny chose to park in another spot for some inexplicable reason. If that would happen, then Ken would have to drive past Danny's parked vehicle, lower the window, and then shoot him from the car. A "drive-by" shooting would be just as good; he just had to make deadly certain that he didn't miss, and that neither the fiancée nor the giant friend had a chance to get involved.

That plan was probably the best for catching Danny alone, however briefly. Whether it was a surprise ambush or a casual drive-by, it should work, and Ken could quickly drive off, exiting in the back of the parking lot. He had checked his escape route thoroughly and would employ a tactic similar to what he had done back in Muncy, Pennsylvania. After a few blocks of back streets, he could get onto Highway 72 heading east. Within a few minutes, however, he would turn left on Elk Rapids Road, a secondary route heading north.

Anyone in pursuit would assume that he was going out of

Traverse City on 72, heading toward I-75, or U.S. 27, or U.S. 131...all of which were divided highways that could take him south. Instead, he would continue to head north on county roads, working his way to Mackinaw City and the Mackinac Bridge. It would only be about 100 miles, five miles across the "Mighty Mac," and then less than an hour to Sault Ste. Marie. Using the John Jacobs false ID that no one knew about, he had bought a plane ticket out of the Chippewa County International Airport there, departing at 11:15 Friday night. The timing was close, but easily doable. He would again park the rental car in the company's return lot, drop the keys in the deposit box, and go right to the gates of the small airport with his duffle.

Ken knew that he would have to stay away from Muncy, Pennsylvania, from the prison, and more to the point, from his dear Sarah, but he would use another inmate's spouse with whom he had become friendly over about two years to get a message to her. Initially, the only communication would be: "Rejoice! It's done." If prison authorities somehow intercepted his message and interrogated her about it, she could easily employ her stubborn resistance and claim not to know what it meant. "A fall apple pie, perhaps? I hope it has a file in it." He imagined with great satisfaction how she would lean back in her chair while being questioned about it, with a hardened smirk on her face, and they would know that she knew about Danny's long-deserved demise, but no one could connect her to the deed. And when pressed about her brother's whereabouts, she could honestly say that she had no idea where he was. It was best that she didn't know.

He would keep in touch with Sarah from time to time, using the other inmate's spouse as a messenger so long as it worked without detection. Then he would turn his attention to legal process to win her release eventually. An extremely well-paid lawyer would work every angle in the appeal process and the parole board avenue. Most promising perhaps was the contention that despite expert testimony at her trial that she had killed her husband, Bill Brand, in a severely diminished mental state, whether temporary insanity or some other diagnosis, she had been found guilty and sentenced in a gross miscarriage of justice. Also worth pursuing was more expert witness testimony that she had suffered mental, psychological and tortuous emotional abuse from a cruel husband and had kept it secret from the outside world due to shame and humiliation.

Much deeper research than had been done before her trial would uncover notes or letters from Bill to her when they had been fighting over her unrestrained spending, threatening to "cut her off," or seize her credit cards. More, well-paid, willing witnesses could be fabricated to testify to their knowledge of his abusive treatment of victim Sarah. More could be done to enlist the involvement of well-meaning domestic abuse advocacy groups, even high-profile feminist groups. If crafted well enough, the appeal process could even win a new trial for her and secure a not-guilty verdict. Failing that, the parole board could be deluged by input that would greatly influence a decision to grant parole and release her. Ken was totally convinced that enough time and effort, an absolute commitment to her cause, would someday result in Sarah becoming a free woman again, and that they would be reunited. And Daniel Henriks would be moldering in his grave. Poor Sarah had been unwise and victimized by her choice of men, but she would always have her devoted brother to watch out for her and protect her.

Ken made his way back to the backwoods farm house and his room there feeling almost smug satisfaction. He had a strong, immediate plan that should result in Danny's death in only a bit more than a week, followed by his undetected escape. He had a long-term strategy that he could devote all of his time and energy to with the goal of winning Sarah's freedom. It was time to put the pieces in place. He would begin by attending the gun show at the Wexford County Fairgrounds in Cadillac, Michigan, this coming Saturday. There he could find the weapon he needed and extra dollars "under the table" should make the purchase untraceable. The next couple of days he would keep his landlady delighted by doing some of those chores he had promised her. It was best to keep busy and continue to lie low until the time was at hand.

CHAPTER FORTY-FOUR

The gun show was a very interesting phenomenon in American culture and society. There was table after table, booths galore, with all manner of handguns, shotguns, rifles, knives, tomahawks, swords, antique weaponry, ammunition, gun powder, lead shot and bullets. The array was virtually dizzying in size and assortment. A large crowd was in attendance, milling around, looking, hefting guns and dickering with dealers, all accompanied by John Phillip Sousa band music from the speakers, interspersed with more modern favorites like "Proud to Be an American" and "Born in the USA."

Ken strolled casually through the enthusiastic crowd, going by the tables and booths perusing the guns on display. From time to time someone would pass him going in the opposite direction with a shotgun or rifle over his shoulder and a tag or sign dangling, "For Sale." He was in no hurry; he would know the right weapon when he saw it. And suddenly he found it.

At a booth with a large sign that proudly said, "America Remembers," he saw a fancy-looking, gold metal handgun with an accompanying sign that said, "Texas Ranger Tribute

Revolver – Only 300 Made." It was commemorative of the long history of the Texas Rangers and their famous "six-shooters," a .45 caliber revolver with a 5 ½ inch barrel made by Colt. He asked the dealer if he might pick it up and feel the balance in his hand.

"Sure, go ahead. It's a beauty, only been fired a few times. It would be a great addition to anyone's collection," the man beamed. Part of his eagerness was the high price on the tag attached to the trigger guard. It would boost his receipts for the day considerably.

Ken thought to himself, *Yes, this would be a great addition all right...to end Henriks' sorry life.* He felt such a gun would be almost poetic. Just as the famed Texas Rangers fought and shot to protect American settlers on the Southern Plains, with this gun and his lifelong admiration of the Rangers he could protect his poor, mistreated sister. He turned the gun to look at the inscribed words on the backstrap of the handle. It read: "They Knew Their Duty and They Did It." *As Perfect as God in His heavens* Ken smiled broadly. This was definitely the right weapon for his mission. He didn't care an iota about dickering.

"Sold," he told the man on the other side of the table, "and here's another C-note to keep it strictly between you and me." When he left with his acquisition in its commemorative wooden case and a box of .45 cartridges, both the men were very pleased with the transaction. Now all Ken needed was patience and a clear target, which would present itself in less than two weeks. The next several days would be delightful in his relaxation and anticipation.

CHAPTER FORTY-FIVE

After Andrea had flown back to Northern Michigan on that Saturday, a week before Ken's successful purchase at the Cadillac Gun Show, Danny had led worship services at South Presbyterian Church that Sunday. He had also suggested that Tim could take that morning off, so closely following Mark's memorial service, but again Tim preferred to be back to work, a decision that resulted in person after person coming up to him before the first service, in between services, and following the second service, to express their condolences and heartfelt prayers.

Although it was emotionally straining, it was also good therapy. He felt loved and supported by so many good members and friends. Despite their noisiness, the PUPs were a small group of fundamentalist zealots, while most of the South Presbyterian members were much more inclusive and understanding and accepting, and they shared his pain and sense of loss over the tragic death of Mark. Most were inclined to assume that it was Buck, Bob, or someone else among the PUPs who was responsible for the shooting, lashing out in their hatred of gays and their fanatic opposition to same-sex marriage. But it was not openly discussed, especially so close to the time of the tragedy. Danny, of course, had established that it was not one of them, a fact confirmed eventually by the police investigation that exonerated the Gibson's and their PUPs.

Danny talked once a day or more with Andrea by phone, keeping her in the loop with the lack of progress in finding Ken Romano, but also assuring her of his safety and watchfulness. He also gave her a daily update on Angela's recovery. She was not only in a regular hospital room, but she was walking and doing a daily therapy program designed to re-strengthen her lung function. Her progress was so encouraging that her primary care physician talked to Tiny and her about likely discharge in the fourth week of September...with very limited activity once she was home with Tiny. Neither of them told the doctor that "very limited activity" would mean driving all the way to Northern Michigan at the end of the month, within a week or so of her discharge. The first Saturday of October Tiny would be getting her "to the church on time," and into his arms for the rest of their lives as Ms. Angela Jones.

The first week that Andrea was back to work and on patrol was extremely busy for her, as well as for Danny, who picked up as much of the pastoral ministry work load as possible to make things less stressful for Tim. The days of that week just sped by and were made busier by the fact that Danny had to go to the hospital daily to visit Angela and Tiny and get Angela's ideas and decisions regarding their upcoming wedding. There were long and loving phone conversations with Andrea, who would give her input for their wedding day and arrangements. Since Angela was stuck in Pittsburgh with Tiny, it fell to Andrea to work things out at her Grand Traverse Presbyterian Church for the rehearsal on the first Friday of October, and, of course, the wedding day itself on the following Saturday.

On Wednesday of that week, two weeks before Danny, Tiny and Angela would drive back up to Northern Michigan, and the same day that Ken scouted out the church, they made plans to call Andrea in the evening from Angela's hospital room. Since Tiny had secured that private room for her, they were able to put the call on speaker, so that all three of them could hear Andrea and talk to her.

"Angie," Andrea said, "I hear your recovery is coming along just great."

"I'm doing much better," she confirmed. "And our guys have been at my beck and call."

"You better believe it," Tiny added, without the least tone of complaint. Being at Angela's service was his number one priority in life, and he intended to keep doing it.

"I'm pleased to report," Andrea continued, "that things are all lined up at the church for our first Saturday in October at 1:30. Rehearsal will be Friday at 7:30 that evening. I've ordered bouquets for us, boutonnieres for our men, smaller bouquets for Lucy and Julie in our fall colors of yellow and orange, and booked the church fellowship hall for our reception. As we discussed before, that seemed easier than trying on such short notice for a large room at a fancy restaurant."

"And a lot cheaper, too," Danny jumped in.

"Pinching the pennies already," Tiny ribbed him.

"Hey, somebody has to," Danny protested. "Not everyone can afford a suite at the downtown Hilton." He wondered to himself if he should have blurted out with that, given that Angela's wounding at Tim and Mark's wedding had prevented Tiny and her from completing their stay at the suite Tiny was so proud of booking for her.

"Well, I think that sounds great," Angela said cheerfully. "It'll be perfect...especially with Big Tiny as my groom." She beamed up at him with that beautiful smile that always made him feel weak in his football-injured knees. "What about the wedding reception lunch?"

"We're having that catered by the helpful folks at Classic Food Catering right on Front Street. Ladies at the church will help with setup, take down, and other tasks, but that seemed easiest, leaving the food prep up to the professionals. And we don't need those cute favors we talked about making. We should keep it simple and as stress-free as possible."

"I agree," Angela replied. "I'm so sorry that all of this has to fall on you, Andrea."

"Hey, no problem," Andrea assured them. "If I can get Danny squared away and toeing the line, a little thing like wedding arrangements is a snap."

They all laughed at that, especially Tiny, who roared as usual, knowing from Danny's sharing with him how Andrea had brought Danny up short with "I'm not sticking around for a 'maybe.'" She was absolutely right. For her, Danny toed the line...and liked it.

"Hey, guys," Danny said to Angela and Tiny, "okay with you if I finish this call out in the waiting area?"

Tiny nodded slowly with a big grin, "Sure, go ahead, lover boy. We don't need to hear all your mush," he kidded Danny.

Angela and Tiny gave Andrea warm goodbyes and "love you's" and Danny took his cell phone down the hall.

"I've been following extreme caution," he assured Andrea, "and while there's been absolutely no trouble from Ken, neither does anyone in any police agency have any idea where he is right now."

"I know," Andrea said, "the investigation is completely cold and dead up here in Northern Michigan. Wes Smith had absolutely nothing more to contribute. Guess we can't do anything but keep waiting and watching." Danny had to agree.

CHAPTER FORTY-SIX

Finally, on the last Friday of September Angela was discharged from the hospital. The doctors had discussed having her stay and continue to do physical and respiratory therapy, but she was adamant that she could recuperate better at home and would keep up with her breathing exercises to strengthen her lung functions. Besides, after three weeks of being hospitalized, the confinement and restrictions were all she could bear.

"Get me out of here," she had insisted tongue-in-cheek with Tiny, who, of course, would have carried her out the door that instant if she had been really serious. As it was, he practically took over pushing her wheelchair down and out the main entrance, except that a diminutive but feisty elderly volunteer said that it was *her* job, thank you. He had plants and floral arrangements and her take-home bag and an abundance of "get-well" cards to carry, anyway.

He took her home to be with him, naturally, and was going to set her up in his relatively-unused dining room downstairs so that she didn't have to climb stairs to lie down or go to bed for the night, but she again insisted that she needed the exercise of using the stairs, and besides, she wanted to be in *his* bedroom. Well, that's what he wanted, too, and actually would have carried her up and down every few minutes if need be.

Together they both rested over the weekend and kept working conscientiously at her therapy. They went out morning and evening for short, casual walks down his block. Tiny lived in one of the better, two-story, brick homes in his section of the Hill District in Pittsburgh. He was known and respected by everyone throughout the entire Hill, many of whom remembered him fearfully from back in his old street gang days and when his business activities were mostly illegal. But he had also given a lot to the people on the Hill. He had stood up for them in the face of Pittsburgh City Administration efforts to "re-urbanize" and force thousands of residents out of their homes and apartments, and he had protected "his people" from infiltration on the part of Central and South American gangs that sought to enslave as many as they could to the nastiest and most destructive street drugs.

Thus, Tiny was greeted often on those short walks with recuperating Angela with smiles and sincere comments like:

"Hey man, good to see ya. God bless you, brother," and....

"This must be that fine lady we've been hearing about. Welcome, ma'am."

As well as, "Tiny, we've been having a problem over on Webster Avenue with some young punks. Could you help us out there?"

"Gosh," said Angela at one point, "it reminds me of a scene from one of the *Godfather* movies, like you're Don Corleone or somebody. Are you sure you want to move away from here and live with me up in Suttons Bay?"

"In a heartbeat, sweetheart. I mean, in some ways this will always be home, and I'll probably want to visit on a little vacation once in a while, see how the brothers here are making do, but my life is with you from now on. Besides, I *really* like it where you live and work. We'll be the happiest couple anybody's ever met...promise."

It was, of course, what Angela really wanted to hear, and she squeezed that massive arm and leaned her head against his shoulder in complete contentment. Tiny, if anything, seemed to straighten up even a little taller, and looked as proud and pleased as any man could be.

When the last Monday of the month arrived, they started to pack and prepare for Wednesday's drive to Northern Michigan. Tiny and Danny had decided that they would make a two-car convoy for the trip – Danny driving his Grand Cherokee, and Tiny taking Angela in his big, black Lincoln. That way, after their wedding each couple could have their own honeymoon transportation. They had decided to spend a few days together as a foursome on Mackinac Island at the famous Grand Hotel and enjoy the sights, sounds, and definitely the tastes of that marvelous resort island, but they would each take several days to be by themselves as well.

The first and second weeks of October would typically be height of the fall color season in the Northern Lower Peninsula and the Upper Peninsula and would present spectacular scenes that would seem like heaven had come to earth.

Tiny and Angela had decided that she could show him the distinctive shops and tourist attractions in Mackinaw City, Petoskey, Charlevoix, and that whole stretch of what has become known as Michigan's "Gold Coast," while Andrea wanted to take Danny north and west in the Upper Peninsula to see Tahquamenon Falls, the Pictured Rocks at Munising, and down to the remarkable Big Spring, "Kitch-iti-kipi," outside Manistique. They would reunite after almost a week and a half back in Traverse City and Suttons Bay.

Beyond an occasional anxious wondering and mental

"head scratching," not a lot of thought was given by the four to the whereabouts and intentions of Kenneth Romano...and certainly no possibility conceived of that he would somehow try to crash a second wedding.

CHAPTER FORTY-SEVEN

The Grand Cherokee-Lincoln Town Car convoy drove west out of Pennsylvania, across most of northern Ohio, and then turned north into Michigan. The farther north they went, the more beautiful autumn color they saw there in the beginning of October: bright red and orange maples, golden yellow aspen, scarlet sumac bushes on the interstate roadside banks, orange-brown sassafras, oak trees still mostly green but showing splashes of deep mahogany and yellow-brown. Whether people prefer to think about the spectacular natural palette scientifically as the dying off of the green chlorophyll, revealing the other colors contained in the leaves...or liked to imagine in childlike wonder the painting of the leaves by Jack Frost...or the smearing of the leaves by the spirits of painted Native Americans, it was the most gorgeous time of the year in the Great Lakes State. And it was the perfect time for their wedding.

They were blessed with a bright and sunny Wednesday for their trip and stopped a couple of times at rest areas with overlooks to take in the rolling hills blanketed with color and interspersed by deep blue lakes. But Andrea was waiting, so they pressed on and arrived in Traverse City in time to meet her for a late supper back at the Mackinaw Brewing Company restaurant. She had time to go to her condo and change out of her uniform and charmed Danny all over again with her combination of a blue Merino wool sweater that hugged her trim body, khaki pants with chukka boots and her favorite Petoskey stone pendant and Leland blue earrings. Danny looked and barely spotted that little bump in the ankle of her right pant leg that indicated she was continuing to pack the little Sig Sauer.

It felt to both of them as if they had been apart for two and a half years rather than mere weeks, and they embraced and kissed deeply. Andrea immediately turned then to Angela and Tiny.

"Wow, look at you, girl, ambulatory and everything. How do you feel?"

"Kinda tired after our long drive today, but I have to say, Tiny's big Lincoln is pretty comfortable riding. I could even recline and snooze when I felt drowsy, although I hated to do so and end up missing all this spectacular color. It is just breath-taking up here."

"I know," Andrea agreed. "It's my favorite time of the year."

"And a great time to get married," Tiny chimed in enthusiastically. He could hardly wait another day.

Andrea loved Danny more than anything, but she sure loved Big Tiny, too, and she stepped up to him and was immediately lost in his enveloping arms. Nobody could bear hug like Tiny. Danny looked on as Angela joined in the bear hug and he came to the overpowering realization that he was looking at his Family...and he felt tremendous joy.

Their reunion supper was delicious, and their excited talk was even better. All was in place for the wedding. Tomorrow, the first Thursday of the month, Andrea and Angela would meet a final time with the caterer and touch base with the ladies at the church who were eagerly helping with all the setup in the Fellowship Hall. They would check their wedding outfits, of course, and take dresses to the cleaners if there was need for any spot removal or final pressing. Even though it was a relatively small and simple wedding, there seemed to be a myriad of little details to check and make sure of.

Danny and Tiny mentally stepped back just a bit, felt dizzied by the women's activity, and primarily made sure that they could instantly respond with "Yes, dear" whenever they heard "Honey, would you please...?" Even though Danny had performed a few hundred weddings as an officiating pastor, and truly appreciated the fact that a lot went into preparing for weddings – including on the church end of it all – like Tiny, he would have been glad just to say, "I do." before Andrea's pastor and get on with the honeymoon.

After supper and a lot of catching up among the four, Tiny drove Angela up to her apartment in Suttons Bay, and Danny followed Andrea in his Jeep to her condo. He carried his bags up to her unit, put them in her bedroom, and then joined her for a nightcap. Of course, she had his Crown Royal Black and her favorite Boskydel Red out on her counter with glasses, awaiting their arrival.

"Sounds like Angela and you have a busy day planned for tomorrow," Danny said. "Do you want me to join in at any point?"

"Nah, I think we can handle it. Actually, I'll do most of the running around, include her for what she especially wants to do, but I think she should get a good amount of rest. Despite her good spirits, today's trip had to wear her out, so a day of mostly rest and refueling would probably be best. She'll certainly want to be reenergized for Friday's rehearsal and Saturday."

"So Tiny and I can kick back and chill out tomorrow?" Danny said hopefully.

"Oh-h no," Andrea brought him up short. "You guys have to make sure your suits are unpacked and freshly pressed. We're not about to have the two of you standing up in front of the church looking like you slept in your suits the whole way across the upper Midwest. Drop them off at my cleaners on the west end of Front Street; they're expecting you first thing in the morning so they can take care of it for you to pick up later that afternoon. Then you need to drive over to The Blossom Shop on E. 8th to pay for the corsages, bouquets and boutonnieres and a center arrangement for the chancel of the church and the buffet table at the reception. They'll deliver the whole order to the church Saturday morning. And while you're there, change the boutonniere order from carnations to fall mums, and please make sure they match the ladies' flowers."

"Copy Central will have our wedding programs for the service, and since they're on 8th also, you can pick those up before or after you get the flowers taken care of. The programs have to go to the church, of course. Also, touch base with Lieutenant Wade and Angela's boss, Sam. Here are their phone numbers. Since I politely declined the lieutenant's offer to walk me down the aisle, I asked if he would stand up with us instead and be a witness. Also, since Sam's wife Julie agreed to be matron of honor with Angela, she and I figured Sam could also stand up and be our witness. Both of them were delighted to be included. They know they need to be at both the rehearsal Friday night at 7:30 and an hour in advance of the 1:30 wedding. But be sure to remind them and have them gather with you in the church office at least a half hour before the service. We women will be using the Church Parlor."

"Oh, while you're out and about tomorrow doing those

drop-offs and pick-ups, you can stop by Gauthier's Shoes & Repair on West Bayshore and they'll give the shoes Tiny and you will be wearing a professional shine. They'll do it on the spot, so anytime is convenient. Here is a list of your appointed tasks so that you don't have to remember it all. I made it short. So it won't be overwhelming. And you can enjoy your day."

Danny stood there, stunned. He was afraid that his mouth dropped with every item Andrea ticked off. He looked feebly at the to-do list and the note with the names and phone numbers, then up at Andrea, smiled weakly, and responded appropriately, "Yes, dear." It was a wonder his fiancée hadn't already been promoted to be Colonel and Director of the Michigan State Police. Organization, administration, and executive action were clearly her fortes. As he had appreciated from first meeting her, Andrea Wilkins, soon-to-be Henriks, was a strong woman.

Orders of the day for tomorrow securely tucked away in his pocket, Danny ventured to change the subject to their ongoing worry about Ken Romano.

"Ken hasn't surfaced or made so much as a peep since he disappeared from the Sunset Motel outside Muncy," he noted. "Maybe he took off and gave up on shooting me. He could even have left the country for all anybody knows. Maybe he found refuge in Samoa since Sarah wasn't able to do so as she had hoped."

"Unfortunately," Andrea replied, "we have no way of knowing. I'm wearing a navy-blue pantsuit instead of a dress for Friday's rehearsal, so I can still wear my ankle holster with my Sig Sauer, just in case. I won't have it for the wedding service, of course, but in addition to Lieutenant Wade, there should be a dozen or so of my fellow troopers in attendance. At least a couple of them will be on duty, in uniform and fully armed – well aware of the potential threat

– so there should be plenty of protection and deterrent should Ken want to try again."

"You don't think he would try to crash another wedding, do you?" Danny asked skeptically. "He's already done that once and failed, so it doesn't seem likely he'd try that again."

Andrea hoped with all her might that he was right, but there was no way to know.

CHAPTER FORTY-EIGHT

Thursday was a flurry of activity for Danny and Tiny as they executed their orders for the day as issued by Andrea. Andrea efficiently took care of the things that were on the women's list, while taking breaks with Angela for morning lattes, lunch, a rest period at her condo in early afternoon, and a coffee date with the boys in late afternoon to check on everyone's progress.

"We're doing well," she pronounced. "It's all coming together as planned."

"Just following orders," Danny grinned, as Tiny looked upon Andrea with an even greater measure of respect...and upon Angela with absolute love.

"And Andrea has made sure that I paced myself and got rest breaks, so I'm holding up well," Angela assured Tiny.

"Now drink up there, guys, you still have to make it back to the cleaners by 5:00 to pick up those suits. You got those shoes shined, right?"

"Yes, dear," Danny teased. "Although Tiny's are so large, I thought they would send us down to the marina for boat scrubbing and barnacle removal." He leaned over, away from his best friend, and flinched as the back of a giant hand whacked his shoulder, although Tiny couldn't help but laugh also.

The four decided to go their separate ways for the evening, including quiet suppers at home, partly to keep Angela from having to go out yet again. They each really wanted some alone time with their spouse-to-be, anyway.

Friday morning Andrea and Angela had hairstyling appointments with manicures and pedicures that would keep them occupied, and Danny and Tiny likewise got haircuts to be able to look their sharpest. The four got together for a late lunch – big burgers and fries at Boone's Prime Time Pub in Suttons Bay, which was convenient for Angela to get back to her apartment nearby with Tiny for a good, long nap and quiet rest of the afternoon. Toward the end of the afternoon they would dress for the rehearsal and meet Danny and Andrea once again at the Mackinaw Brewing Company for a light supper. Tiny decided he would order the walleye sandwich this time. He still hadn't tired of the great freshwater fish choices.

Danny and Andrea likewise spent their afternoon at her condo, also catching their breath and leaning back and relaxing, as Danny had hoped for earlier.

"You've done a great job pulling all this together, my love," he said to Andrea with much sincerity. God, how he admired and loved this woman.

"A labor of love, my love," she smiled that gorgeous smile that always melted him to the core, "a labor of love."

"You realize that all I really needed was you and me and your pastor, standing before God and pledging our eternal commitment to each other," Danny assured her.

"Yah, me, too. But it will be a lovely little wedding, and how great that the four of us can do this together. And how amazing that we'll all make our lives together here in this marvelous Grand Traverse area. My cherished childhood home will be made complete as I never expected it could be, thanks to our going to the range that Sunday and getting ourselves shot at," she laughed.

"Well, technically, it was *I* who was shot at; you just happened to be standing in front of me as the bullet whizzed between us."

"Hey, I could have been shot, you know," Andrea protested as she threw a lounge chair pillow at him playfully. "We're both lucky he wasn't a better shot...or was it Providence?"

"I've always depended upon guardian angels," Danny replied with a serious tone. Then he switched topics to their planned life together. "Tiny was pleasantly surprised when I told him that I was going to move here, too. As you know, he had already decided to sell his businesses in Pittsburgh, turn things over to Slick, Speed, and the rest of his boys, and start a little, initially at least, one-man security business in this area. He's done well back there in Pittsburgh and Angela wants to keep doing what she's doing, so their income will be fine for the modest lifestyle they have in mind."

"And as you also know," Danny continued, "I've talked long-distance with the Mackinac Presbytery Office in Petoskey. I had interim pastor training some years ago, before I was called to be pastor at South Presbyterian, and they always have some small church up here in Northern Michigan that needs a temporary pastor. I've served long enough to be able to take my own early retirement, draw a good pension from the denomination, and it won't matter for us whether any temporary position is full-time or part-time. And if it's some distance away, like up in the UP, I can work my schedule so as to split my weeks between that community and here."

"Well, I can't tell you how grateful I am that you're so willing to do that and enable me to continue my career with the state police. Lieutenant Wade has assured me that given my exemplary record, what else would you expect?" she kidded, but Danny took her with utmost seriousness, "he'll have no trouble keeping me at the Post on 14th Street. It's nothing but miraculous how we are provided for."

"You know," Danny offered, "your condo here is comfortable for the two of us. You have a guest room and a third room for a study that we can share. This balcony is great. A nice view, trees and birds, even your hummingbirds coming to your feeder. If you would rather, we could have a perfectly good home right here, and I can just sell my house and stuff back in Pittsburgh."

"Uh, uh, Buster," she shot back, "you promised me a yard and a bird dog, and I'm holding you to it. While you're resigning and terminating your pastorate there in Pittsburgh, I'm leading our charge to house shop in this Grand Traverse area. Maybe we can find something nice up there in the Suttons Bay area, be close to Angela and Tiny."

Truth be known, Danny thought to himself, *a house with a yard and a bird dog was something we both agreed would be nice the very first time we met, but it was never actually a promise.* But there was no quibble room in this matter, besides, it was what he really wanted, too. He was just giving Andrea the option not to have to give up her attractive condo.

Late afternoon had arrived on this warm October day, so they showered together, expressed their love for each other, got dressed for the supper with Tiny and Angela, and looked forward to their rehearsal at the church. They had no idea the rehearsal would have to be postponed.

CHAPTER FORTY-NINE

After another fun meal at Mackinac Brewing Company from 6:00 to 7:00, Danny, Tiny, Andrea and Angela drove to the Presbyterian Church on the east side of Traverse City. As Danny always wanted, they pulled into the church parking lot at precisely 7:15. Several cars were already there, including the pastor's, the organist's, Julie and Sam's, Lucy's, and a few others they didn't recognize, probably the custodian's, and a dark blue Ford sedan in the first stall nearest the main doors of the church.

"Oh, there's Lucy, Julie and Sam," Angela said with delight as she saw them chatting just outside the door, about to go in. Park right next to that blue car," she suggested, not wanting to be a backseat driver, but just eager to dash over and greet her friends.

Ken immediately felt a surge of uncertainty as he peered over the bottom of the passenger side window of his blue rental car. A black Lincoln Town Car was slowly pulling into the parking lot. He had been certain that he would be seeing Danny's Grand Cherokee just about this time. Had the wedding party rented a formal sedan for their weekend? The windows were tinted darkly so that he couldn't make out who was driving or who was sitting where in the luxurious car. Or maybe it wasn't them at all; maybe some rich relative was coming to the rehearsal. In any case, he had to be ready, so his left hand was on the door handle, his right hand holding the .45 revolver, poised to fire. He was ready to step out very fast.

Tiny swung his Lincoln into the parking stall next to the blue car as Angela asked, making sure that there was plenty of space between the two, not wanting to have his gleaming black paint job scratched by a dreaded parking lot incident. He turned off his motor, swiveled his head around to their ladies in the back seat, and joked, "Well, here we are, next to last chance to back out...Not!"

He swung the door open and got out of the driver's side to step back and open the door for Angela. At the same time, Danny exited the front passenger side, also stepping back to open the door for Andrea.

Simultaneously with Tiny emerging from the Lincoln, Ken swung his passenger door open, lunged out...and was surprisingly confronted not by his intended target, Danny, but by a giant of a man face-to-face with him only a couple of feet away. Startled and panicked in the split-second encounter, his trigger finger squeezed before he could even swing the revolver up, grazing Tiny's left leg. It was a slight, superficial wound, but enough to cause Tiny to stagger just a bit, while swinging his right fist toward Ken's face. Without Tiny being tilted off balance, the blow would probably have knocked Ken senseless, but as it was, it glanced off the top of his head, but with enough force to land him on his back.

Meanwhile, Danny had opened the door for Andrea, who was stepping out from the back seat just as she heard the misguided shot, accompanied by Tiny's bellow of pain and rage. All in one motion, she pushed Danny down along the passenger side of the car, drew her Sig Sauer from her ankle holster, and quickly had it up in both hands, taking aim.

As Tiny regained his balance and lurched to seize the cowardly bastard, Ken scrambled to his feet by the back of the Taurus, swinging his head in the direction of Andrea coming around the back of the Lincoln, gun drawn and taking aim. As he backpedaled to keep out of reach of the lunging Tiny, he snapped off a shot in the direction of Andrea, missing badly. Andrea could have fired back, but realized that behind Ken, in the direction of the main door of the church, Sam, Julie, and Lucy were now scrambling to try to find safety.

Andrea barked at Tiny, "Tiny, get down, Now! I can't get a shot." Amazingly, Tiny was able to restrain his adrenaline-fueled fury and drop to one knee at the back corner of the Ford as Andrea charged forward. But Ken in his panic made it around to his driver's side, jumped into the driver's seat, and hit the ignition. He turned and aimed his gun in their direction.

Andrea was then able to squeeze off a shot, with nothing but trees in the background, and the bullet went through the back window, but deflected just a little by the impact, narrowly missed Ken's head and exited the car through the front windshield, making holes and spider-webbed cracking in both sheets of glass.

As the car's engine caught, Danny had come running around, saw that Ken was about to floor it, and reaching down with more strength than he knew he had, grabbed Tiny's collar, and yanked him out of the way of the backward-hurtling car. Andrea jumped out of the way, still taking aim and ready to fire a second round but held up because of houses in the background to the side of the parking lot.

Ken managed to roar off, leaving black rubber marks on the asphalt, and careened out the back exit of the parking lot, turning east. Andrea grabbed her cell to call in to 911 to have a dragnet and roadblocks set up ASAP, but at the same time assessing the state of her loved ones at the scene.

Angela came running out from the driver's side back seat, where she had been blocked in by the furious action, saw Tiny still kneeling, his pant leg torn, and blood dripping onto the asphalt.

"Oh my God! Oh my God," she wailed, "Tiny, are you okay? You're bleeding. Somebody call an ambulance. Andrea, please call." Andrea had already done so and told her.

Danny meanwhile shouted over to the church entrance as Sam, Julie, Lucy, and now the pastor, were hesitantly coming out from the sanctuary of the church building, "Quick, grab some clean towels and a first-aid kit if you can find one." The pastor was able to find a kit in the church office, and he told Julie where she could find white tea towels in a drawer in the front narthex of the church, where Sunday morning coffee hour was always held.

Within just a couple of minutes, both Danny and Andrea were swabbing the bullet graze with alcohol patches, wiping away blood, keeping pressure on the site, and wrapping gauze bandages around Tiny's tree-like calf.

"It's just a scratch," he insisted. "I'll be fine."

As the two treated him, they could hear sirens approaching from both an ambulance and Traverse City Police cars. In an instant the authorities would be on the scene.

CHAPTER FIFTY

An enraged Tiny didn't want to wait and lose time having their statements taken, having his bullet graze examined by EMT's, hanging around while police investigators looked for evidence.

"I want to go after him," Tiny growled. "Anybody with me?"

Andrea, Angela, and Danny looked around at each other. Danny insisted that he go, not willing to have Tiny charge ahead alone.

"Well, somebody has to stay here to meet with the police," Andrea pointed out.

Tiny turned to Angela, "Will you do that, hon? I just don't want him to get away again."

Angela nodded her assent but insisted that Tiny be careful and not approach Ken or put himself in harm's way. Tiny agreed, all the while thinking that if he could only get Ken within reach again, he would snap the coward's neck like a pretzel.

"I'll go, too," Andrea insisted. "I'm the one with a gun."

The thought crossed both Danny's mind and hers that she could possibly get in trouble as an off-duty state police officer not waiting for the city police to arrive and begin their investigation, but since Ken was surely headed toward M72, a state highway, he may already be in state police jurisdiction, where her involvement and that of her fellow troopers would become primary. In any case, as the sirens were about to reach the church, the three hustled into Tiny's Lincoln and sped off, Danny driving since Tiny's leg was pretty sore. They had helped him into the back seat where he could spread out and ease the pain of the wound.

Danny headed in the same direction that Ken had taken, and within a few blocks turned east on M72 going out of Traverse City. Meanwhile, Andrea was calling again to her Post dispatcher, informing the state patrol cars that the suspect appeared to be heading east, possibly toward U.S. Highway 131. Danny pushed the powerful Lincoln above the posted speed limits. As they sped east, they anxiously scanned ahead for any sight of the blue Ford.

By the time they got out as far as the Williamsburg Road, Danny said to Andrea and Tiny, "I think I may know where he's heading."

"How could you know that?" Andrea replied. "He has multiple primary routes he can take south on major highways, to say nothing of all the county and township roads going back into the woods. Dispatch reports that they have a roadblock set up near the Kalkaska Post, at 72 and 131, but he could have turned off at any number of places before then."

"I don't think he's going south," Danny asserted. "That would be too obvious – that he would want to drive back to Pennsylvania, or home to Texas. Remember that they couldn't find a trace of him back in Pennsylvania, after he fled from Muncy. The supposition was that he drove in an unexpected direction and then hopped a flight, obviously now, to Michigan. He's very likely heading north, to throw off pursuers again."

Tiny spoke up from the back seat, "Where would he fly out from up here, now that he's left Traverse City?"

Andrea knew the possibilities. "The closest and best possibility would be at the Pellston Regional Airport farther north of here. But it's a fairly small airport, and we can easily seal him off from there with our BOLO."

Danny offered an alternative. "I think he always has a backup plan, and where could he go to the north and have a good alternative option?"

"Sault Ste. Marie?" Andrea guessed.

"I think so," Danny agreed. "Sure, it's a good deal farther, and he has to cross the Mackinac Bridge to get there, but it's probably only a couple of hours or a bit more for him at this point, and he probably figures that no one would think of that possibility. Besides, if flying out of the Chippewa County Airport doesn't feel right to him, he can probably switch vehicles and make it over the International Bridge into Ontario. It's a guess on my part, but I'd alert the bridge authorities as well as your highway patrol to be on the lookout both at Mackinac and at Sault Ste. Marie."

"I'll get right on it," Andrea assured him.

"So, what do think we should do?" Tiny asked as Andrea was calling back to dispatch.

"I think he's going to be wary about roadblocks at major route intersections like 72 and 131 at Kalkaska. I don't know if it will work, but I'm going to roll the dice here and turn north at Elk Rapids Road," Danny replied, just as he was reaching the corner.

It so happened that Danny was guessing correctly, and as they turned north on Elk Rapids Road, Ken Romano was drawing close to the little town of Elk Rapids, about twelve miles ahead, where he continued north on U.S. Highway 31, a two-lane route, which eventually took him through the attractive tourist destinations of Charlevoix, Petoskey, and eventually to Pellston, where he drove past the small village and its little airport and continued through the night to the junction with Interstate 75, very close to the Big Bridge. Although he had torn out of the church parking lot and down the back streets behind the church, when he had reached 72 and farther on, he had scrupulously kept just a bit above the speed limit, in most places 55 mph, not wanting to draw attention from any law enforcement vehicle.

Danny, behind the wheel of the Lincoln, had been driving faster, so as they approached I-75, they were close behind the Ford, although they hadn't spotted it yet as they drove onto the entrance ramp. It had taken them close to two hours to get there, and he desperately hoped he was right. Very quickly they slowed down a bit to proceed onto the giant suspension bridge, took note of the flashing warning signs about high wind hazard, and continued to scan ahead.

"There, about five cars ahead," Andrea called out. "A dark blue car. It could be him."

And it was.

CHAPTER FIFTY-ONE

After cresting the high point in the bridge between the two main suspension towers, Ken eased downward toward the toll booths just on land at St. Ignace. But as he drew within sight of the booths, he saw red, flashing lights that had to be bridge authority cops...or maybe even Michigan State Police. Each vehicle was being stopped and drivers were being questioned.

For the first time since he had begun his mission to kill Danny, Ken felt trapped. Even if it turned out that they weren't looking for him, the spider-webbed holes in both his windshield and his back window would immediately draw their unwanted attention.

He slowed virtually to a stop, feeling panicky again and desperately looking around for a way out. There was nowhere to go ahead; it was far too high to get out and jump off the bridge support, and it was one-way traffic in the direction he was heading.

Nonetheless, he had space around him as the bridge traffic was light, approaching 10:00 at night, so hoping he could do so before the authorities up ahead noticed him, he actually did a U-turn, bumped over the concrete divider and headed south, back up the sloping deck of the bridge. He had just started to drive south when he stopped at the sight of an oncoming car on the other side...a big, black, Lincoln Town Car.

In a split-second, Ken's panicky feelings bounced from feeling inescapably trapped to one of irrational delight. God was surely favoring his righteous cause in support of his mistreated sister, Sarah, for however improbably, his target had been delivered back into his reach. He screeched to a stop, threw open the driver's door, clutched his Texas Ranger Tribute Revolver, and stepped out into gale-like winds that seemed to have increased since he had started the bridge crossing.

Not about to repeat his previous mistake, instead of firing at the form behind the wheel, undoubtedly the big, black man, Ken snapped off a shot toward the passenger's side of the windshield. And although Andrea had been sitting there, as soon as they had driven up and been confronted by the blue Ford heading toward them in the oncoming lane, she had gotten out, pistol drawn, ready to shoot.

Ken saw her, readying herself behind the open passenger door of the Lincoln, and fired another shot in Andrea's direction, putting a bullet hole in the door panel. Then, as Andrea returned fire with a shot from her Sig Sauer, Ken ran alongside his rental car, looking for a better vantage point to get a clear shot...not only at Andrea, but especially at Danny, and whoever else might be in the Town Car.

He climbed over the railing of the walkway, but in the whipping wind he couldn't balance at the top of the railing to shoot down at Andrea and the occupants of the car. The driver he now recognized as Danny, outside and crouching behind the car door. But it just so happened that the 24.5 inch-thick main suspension cable came down close to deck level at that very point, so he climbed up on it, balancing and grabbing a smaller cable with his left hand to steady himself.

At this higher vantage point Andrea was exposed, as well as his despicable primary target. He didn't care if Andrea fired at him; he swung his precious revolver in Danny's direction and took careful aim as the howling wind whipped at his jacket. At last, he had him.

CHAPTER FIFTY-TWO

The psalmist of the Old Testament wailed in his writing, "How long, O Lord?" How long before God would answer desperate, pleading prayers and Provide mercy, deliverance, and justice? Only God knows the answer to that wailing prayer, but in God's time answers do, in fact, come on earth. God reaches a point in time and events where a divine decision is made that "enough is enough," and the prayer is resolved.

There was wrapped in the gale-like winds that early October night at the Straits of Mackinac the unseen convergence of *three* angels of heaven. It was a spiritual, cosmic event of applied divine power beyond human comprehension or possible description. The angel of Providence and Protection still hovered over Danny, Tiny and Andrea, so that Ken's bullets were deflected off the mark. At the same time, the Angel of Divine Vengeance whisked Ken off his balancing perch with a mere flick that seemed tornadic in its force to the three at the Town Car. And as Ken's flailing body struck the water far below, its impact was met simultaneously by the Angel of Death, who swept the departing soul up and carried it away...but not to the Eternity of Heaven.

Danny, Andrea, and a slightly limping Tiny all fought through the wind to look over the railing. In the darkness it was hard to see, but they could just barely make out the inert form of Ken Romano's body in the water down below. Then he sank beneath the waves. Thoughts and feelings were all mixed up and hard to express, so Danny simply said in the lowering wind, "It's over."

CHAPTER FIFTY-THREE

A state police officer standing outside his patrol car near the toll booth had spotted the Ford as it did its illegal U-turn and headed back up the deck of the bridge. As he called to his partner, they had both seen the nose-to-nose standoff of Ken's car and a big, black sedan. They jumped into their highway patrol car to head that way, and while they couldn't hear the shots because of the howling wind, they could see figures crouching behind open car doors on the Lincoln and a third figure running along the bridge railing. It certainly looked like a shootout was taking place. They immediately radioed for backup from the St. Ignace Post and drew up to the scene, where there were three individuals standing at the railing and looking down at the dark, roiling water.

"All of you, stay where you are. Hands held high where I can see them," hollered the sergeant, his service pistol drawn. "And put the weapon down on the pavement," he bellowed at Andrea, as she carefully complied.

"I'm Highway Patrol Officer Andrea Wilkins, of the Traverse City Post," Andrea identified herself as the sergeant and his partner approached them. "I'll reach slowly for my badge and ID," she suggested, and she soon established her credentials with her fellow state troopers. She helped to verify the identities of Danny and Tiny as well, and together they proceeded to inform the officers that they had been following the very perpetrator for whom the dragnet and road block had been set up.

It took a while, of course, for everything to get sorted out there on the bridge, but as soon as they got the go-ahead, Tiny called Angela to let her know that the three of them were all safe, and that Ken was gone forever. The investigation would have to include searching for Ken's body as soon as practicable with a Coast Guard search and recovery boat. The task would be made somewhat easier now that the strong wind had subsided, but the combination of the dark night and the powerful Straits of Mackinac currents would still make retrieval of the corpse challenging.

While Tiny was on the phone with her, Danny said to both him and Andrea, "Our rehearsal...and we can't call off the wedding."

Tiny relayed Danny's concern to Angela, who assured them, "The pastor is being really flexible and helpful. He suggested that if everything is resolved tonight and nothing prevents us from doing so, we can have a quick and simple rehearsal/run-through late tomorrow morning, take a break to get ready, and still go ahead with the wedding at our planned 1:30 time...but no guns and no shooting. He was very definite about that, 'else it's a deal breaker."

All four of them laughed at that over the phone, the stress, tension, and fear subsiding and flowing away.

CHAPTER FIFTY-FOUR

It was past 2:00 in the morning by the time Danny, Andrea, and Tiny got back to Traverse City. Angela had gotten a ride from the helpful pastor, left the church, and went to Andrea's condo with the extra key Andrea had given her. The three had talked more with her as they headed back south and west from Mackinac, and although Tiny especially had encouraged her to go to bed, or at least lie down and rest, adrenaline and worry had kept Angela up until the Town Car could be seen pulling into a visitor's parking stall outside the condo.

"Oh God, I'm so relieved you're back, and that none of you were hurt any further. What about your leg, my love?" she looked anxiously at Tiny.

"Really, it's just a scratch, a graze. Looks worse than it is, 'cause of all the blood, but I'll be fine. And I'm NOT missing our wedding tomorrow."

"Okay, okay, don't get all riled up, big boy," Andrea scolded him, tongue-in-cheek. "We could still take you to Emergency at Munson, have it looked at. What about a tetanus shot or an anti-biotic to guard against infection?"

"All I want is for all of us to get what rest we can, get up tomorrow morning and get ready and be at the church in time for the wedding," Tiny insisted.

"Well, there'll still have to be paperwork filled out on the incident," Andrea replied, "but since you were never treated by EMT's and have the right to refuse treatment for a minor injury, no one can force you to go to the hospital. I have good first-aid supplies in my bathroom, so let's at least take a look at the wound site, clean it off further with antiseptic, and re-bandage your calf."

"I already got it all out and set it on your kitchen counter," Angela reported. "I had a feeling Tiny wouldn't take the time to go to the hospital. You think it'll be okay?"

"I'm fine. All of you, I tell you, I'm fine. Back on the Hill one time I was so cut up after..." He glanced uncertainly in Angela's direction, "...and my cousin Quincy bandaged me up..." Angela's look of horror and disgust shut him off without further explanation. "Never mind, just clean it up and on to the wedding. 'Get me to the church on ti-i-ime,'" he burst out in his trademark bass.

His deflection worked, causing all of them to laugh at his singing, and no further attention was paid to his old knife-fight story, although Andrea hushed up the three of them.

"Hey, guys, the neighbors. It's 2:30 in the morning, you know."

They had all brought their wedding clothes to Andrea's condo so that they didn't have to rush back and forth to Angela's apartment in Suttons Bay the day of the wedding. Angela joined Andrea in her bedroom for what hours of sleep they could manage; Tiny did a good job of filling the queen-size bed in Andrea's guest room, and Danny had planned on using the pull-out bed in the living room sofa, but as soon as the other three retired he just plopped down on the sofa in his exhaustion and went right to sleep. At least he was no longer a target for sicko Ken to take pot shots at, so he felt no need to try sleeping "with one eye open" anymore.

CHAPTER FIFTY-FIVE

Saturday morning Danny, Andrea, Tiny and Angela took turns getting ready, the women using Andrea's bath, and the men using her guest bath. They went to the Presbyterian Church in Tiny's Lincoln for the 11:00 rehearsal as the pastor had suggested, took a lunch break at noon, and made sure all the arrangements were in order while they enjoyed take-out sandwiches and beverages provided by Classic Food Catering.

Angela and Andrea changed into their wedding dresses and Tiny and Danny into their suits during their break. All was ready when the organ played the traditional "wedding march" at 1:30. The pastor stood facing the congregation in the center; Julie and Lucy were on his right, with Sam and Lieutenant Wade to the left. As they had planned, Andrea and Danny marched down the center-left main aisle, and Angela and Tiny paralleled them down the center-right main aisle. They stood as a foursome throughout the brief Wedding Service.

Initially as they had begun planning their joint wedding, the four all had their personal ideas about the vows they would like to write and say to their new spouses, but as they shared their individual ideas, they had come to a mutual decision that they would each, all four, exchange the same vow, which they had memorized and practiced until each had it perfect. In turn they uttered the name of their spouse and proclaimed:

"I promise, with God's help and God's perfect love, to be your (wife, husband). I will always love you for so long as I live on this earth, and forever in the kingdom of heaven. I will always support you and encourage you in your life and work, in your dreams and goals, and in each day as it unfolds for you and us. I will be ever faithful, forsaking all others, and belong solely to you. You will be constantly in my love and prayers; you will be the center of my life; you will always be beauty and wonder and every good thing to me. You are God's miraculous gift, and for you I will always give thanks, through Jesus Christ our Lord."

The reception in the church Fellowship Hall was joyful, fun, and full of blessings and well-wishing and good food. A mini-flash mob of Andrea's choir buddies gathered around the piano and serenaded the four. Several dances took place on the end of the hall by the piano. By about 3:30 most of the guests had left and Danny and Andrea were hugging her parents and seeing them off for their return home. Sam, Julie and Lucy stayed a little while longer, but soon departed, promising to see the four of them soon after they returned from their honeymoons.

"We did it!" Angela shouted outside the church as they proceeded to Tiny's Town Car to head back to Andrea's condo and change out of their wedding dresses and suits.

"I had no doubts, no doubts at all," Tiny declared. "Nope, nothing could derail this wedding, and now I'm the happiest husband on the planet."

"Hey," Danny protested, "me too, you know. I just married the most wonderful woman God ever created."

"You better believe it, Buster," Andrea added, and Danny was very certain she meant it. Andrea and he locked together for yet another deep kiss.

Since most of their bags were already packed, Tiny and Angela were ready to hit the road shortly after returning to the condo. They waited for Danny and Andrea so that they could Town Car-Grand Cherokee convoy again up to Mackinaw City, take the ferry over to Mackinac Island, and check in at the Grand Hotel, where they would stay in suites for the first three nights of their married lives.

"You realize," he chided Danny, "that for the next week and a half I'm turning the protection service responsibility over to State Trooper Andrea Henriks. I'm going to be extremely unavailable," he smiled and winked.

"She has it well under control," Danny assured him. "Although I find it hard to believe that anyone else could be gunning for me. I think I'm safe now."

Tiny grew serious. "You haven't forgotten that Sarah is still alive and spinning who knows what web there in that prison in Muncy. She's proven herself to be a demonically determined woman."

"You got that right, brother," Danny laughed. "At least if she tries again, she's run out of brothers to do her bidding, so it will cost her big bucks to hire a professional hit man."

Tiny was not amused by his attempt to make light of Sarah's malevolence. "You also remember that she must still have big bucks to draw from. She may be incarcerated, but the authorities have never been able to seize those numbered, offshore accounts Dr. Brand had squirreled away for her before she offed him."

But Danny was not about to let Tiny's concern cast any shadow over their perfect wedding day and the beginning of their respective honeymoons. He still insisted on being tongue-in-cheek about any potential threat to their well-being.

"Hm-m," he smiled. "I wonder if Andrea will be packing her Sig Sauer in her honeymoon outfits? I know there'll be fireworks, at least," he laughed, with Tiny joining in with his big wink and knowing smile.

Angela and Andrea came out; Tiny helped Angie into his car, and they waved goodbye enthusiastically.

"We're right behind you," Danny hollered. "Heading to Mackinaw City tonight."

CHAPTER FIFTY-SIX

Danny got Andrea's luggage and his duffel into his Grand Cherokee and soon they were off. Tiny's Lincoln was up the street a bit, but they would catch up before long.

"Can you believe it?" Danny said to his bride. "Here we are, less than a day later, heading back up to Mackinac."

"I know," Andrea agreed. "It's incredibly surreal. You don't think we should have canceled and changed our honeymoon plans, do you?"

"Not a chance. I'm not about to be held captive to evil and fear. Not even Ken's obsession and Sarah's twisted sickness can spoil the natural beauty and grace up there at the 'Mighty Mac.' And I'm really looking forward to the Grand Hotel on Mackinac Island. I've never been there, but I remember seeing those scenes in that movie, *Somewhere in Time,* and it looks super overlooking Lake Huron. And I understand they have a good breakfast buffet and omelets cooked-to-order tomorrow morning."

"Sounds great," Andrea smiled radiantly. "All I really need and want is you, but I imagine by tomorrow morning I'll like one of those omelets, too."

"I know I will," Danny assured her. "And we can spend

time there on the island before returning to Mackinaw City Wednesday morning, crossing the bridge and heading into the Upper Peninsula. Is there something you'd like to do there in Mackinaw City?"

"I'm going to take you to Colonial Fort Michlimackinac on Wednesday," she declared. "You'll love it. It's one of the best archeological digs and reconstructions you'll find anywhere in the country. It's really interesting, and with the displays and demonstrations and special events, you can spend the whole day there if you want to."

"Right up my alley," Danny agreed. "As a matter of fact, why don't we book a stay at the Hampton Inn for a night, and just spend part of Wednesday and Thursday at the fort and other places there in Mackinaw City. Tahquamenon Falls will still be there a day later, and we'll just change our reservation at the motel outside the State Park."

That settled, as they drove north, they settled into talking about their planned life together.

"Gosh," Danny suddenly remembered as they drove north behind the Lincoln, "with all the excitement as soon as we arrived at the church for the rehearsal, I completely forgot to tell you that while we were getting ready to leave to go to the church, I got a call from the search committee chair for Mackinac Presbytery. It seems that in addition to a church or two that could use me as an interim pastor, they think that my credentials and experience would qualify me well to be a candidate for their interim executive presbyter position."

"Wow, that's great," Andrea exclaimed. "How would that work for us?"

"Well, they said they supposed they could wait to interview me until after our honeymoon..."

"Really big of them," Andrea interrupted, tongue-in-cheek.

"...Yeah, well," Danny went on, "I think they've heard of

you and that you're frequently packing, so don't interfere with her honeymoon," he laughed. Turning serious again, he went on,

"So, I agreed to meet with them at the end of the week after next, on Friday. If they decide they want me, it could be a temporary job for maybe a couple of years. The presbytery office is in Petoskey, which, as you know, is about 65-70 miles from Traverse City, so it's a bit far to commute to the office every day. But I can live wherever I want, and probably arrange my schedule to work from home part of each week."

"But that would be better for us than if you had to go live most of the week near a Presbyterian church in Iron River or someplace else in the western U.P.," Andrea became even more enthused. "And if we end up buying one of those beautiful homes in the East Bay region, the commute would be a lot easier to go to Petoskey."

"That's right," Danny readily agreed. "And after the interim EP job, an East Bay home would put me closer to just about any church I might supply in the northern Lower Peninsula. But if I don't have to drive through Traverse City to get to work, it would be you who would have the commute to your Post on 14th Street, so you would have the traffic."

"No problem," she sniffed. "I am a state trooper, you know; I can handle traffic. As a matter of fact," she laughed, "you should see it when I drive my car to report in at the Post. I'm wearing my uniform, of course, and as cars start to pass me on the left, sometimes going a bit too fast, the driver glances over, sees me in my dark blue uniform, and all of a sudden, he lets up on the gas, slows down, and pulls in behind me, letting me have the right-of-way. One of the little perks of my job," she laughed.

Both of them beamed contentedly and settled back for the rest of their drive up to Mackinaw City. The autumn leaves were right about at peak color and with sunset occurring about quarter-after-7:00, the lowering sun lighted up the banks of fall foliage in a spectacular display. Danny's friend and colleague had it right: this entire region of the country had to be the front porch of heaven itself.

Most beautiful place in America, Danny thought, *and I really am the most blessed new husband in the world.*

"Words can't suffice to capture how miraculous this has been for us, my love. And for Tiny and Angela, too. Despite people wanting to kill me, the past few weeks of God leading me to you has been the greatest thing I could ever want and pray for in my life," Danny declared.

"I know," Andrea agreed wholeheartedly. "There's no other word for it than 'Miraculous' with a capital M. Life itself is a miracle, but I can't think of a bigger miracle than you and me, together always in life and love."

CHAPTER FIFTY-SEVEN

The Angel of Providence and Protection swept over and ahead of Tiny's Town Car and Danny's Grand Cherokee. The envelope of spiritual energy the angel imposed had kept all of the occupants of the cars from having to meet and be gathered up by the Angel of Death during everything that had happened in the last several weeks. The divine protection would continue according to God's right time.

At some time in the future of both Earth and the cosmos each of the four, of course, would have that inevitable appointment with the Angel of Death, who would cradle the souls into the Kingdom of Heaven and the Presence of God Almighty...but not yet, not for some time to come. God's protection for their lives on earth kept the angel at work.

If the angel had a human-like form and visage, it would have smiled and sighed with satisfaction. If it had human-like emotions and pride, it probably would have indulged in a tremendous feeling of self-congratulation. It had been a powerful and particularly intricate application of Divine Providence that had brought Tiny and Angela, Danny and Andrea together almost simultaneously. The fact that each person had fallen in love had been greatly dependent upon their own free will, the choice and decision each of them made, but the weaving of their paths together into a strong spiritual fabric had been an unusually beautiful work of Providence. The angel had provided them opportunity, and each of the four had seized it and chosen Love.

The End

EPILOGUE

Continuing the saga established by *Death Comes to the Rector* and its sequel, *Death Crashes the Wedding*, Book Three in David Q. Hall's *Death Most Unholy* series is entitled *Death Stalks the Forest*. Below is an excerpt:

The Angel of Death soared over the surreal scene on the edge of State Highway 72 in Northern Michigan. Down below, the flashing lights of the Michigan State Police patrol car created a strobe-like effect on the otherwise pitch-black highway.

At shortly after 2:00 in the morning, traffic was very light. The first vehicle to approach the scene was still over the next hill, just starting to climb the far slope.

A rusty, red pickup truck sped away, spraying gravel and leaving the patrol car sitting on the dark roadside. The body of state trooper James Baldwin splayed in front of his car, blood spreading onto the asphalt and the gravel edge.

The angel swept down as Officer Baldwin's fading heart fluttered its final, faint beat, gathered up the soul. It cradled the essence of the dedicated law enforcement officer, faithful husband and loving father of two young girls, and carried him into the eternity of the Kingdom of Heaven. The flashing lights glinted off the handle and the bottom of the long blade left stuck in the chest of the corpse, as the widening pool of blood gave its own bizarre reflections of the red and blue lights.

ABOUT THE AUTHOR

The Rev. Dr. David Quincy Hall is a retired Presbyterian pastor living with his beloved wife, the Rev. Maxine, their daughters, son-in-law, grandson, and two dogs in Oceanside, Southern California.

David is a lifelong civil rights activist, environmentalist, and social justice advocate. His first two experiences in pastoral ministry were in the inner-city areas of San Francisco, California and Pittsburgh, Pennsylvania in the 1960's. He has dialogued with and lobbied members of Congress in Washington, D.C. and state legislators and committees regarding these issues.

His parish ministry was with congregations across the country in Pennsylvania, Michigan, Iowa, Wisconsin and California, in diverse settings including metropolitan, inner city, suburban, medium-sized and small cities, small town, rural, and the North Woods. Firsthand experience living in those different areas provides rich and accurate details for the scenes and settings in his books. Even more, his privilege in working with and serving all kinds of people helps to create characters who are authentic and believable as you meet them.

Death Crashes the Wedding is the second book of the *Death Most Unholy* series. The first book, *Death Comes to the Rector*, was a bestseller in paperback fiction. The third installment is entitled *Death Stalks the Forest*.